Diana woke to find Reid watching her

"Well, Mrs. Lockwood," he said, "How now?"

She knew then that what she was thinking hadn't been a figment of her imagination. Between her first and second nap he had made long, heavenly love to her. "I feel marvelous," she answered lazily.

His gray eyes glinted. "You won't mind repeating the experience?"

She shook her head, blushing. "Supposing someone had seen us?"

"I had a look round beforehand."

"You meant it to happen. Giving me champagne!"

"No, champagne may lower a woman's resistance, but it doesn't heighten her responsiveness. The champagne made you sleepy. Sleeping in the sun is an aphrodisiac."

"Is it? How did you know?" she asked.

Reid didn't answer immediately. "Probably read it somewhere."

But his hesitation made her guess that he had firsthand experience.

ANNE WEALE
is also the author of these

Harlequin Presents

and these

Harlequin Romances

Many of these titles are available at your local bookseller.

For a free catalog listing all available Harlequin Romances
and Harlequin Presents, send your name and address to:

HARLEQUIN READER SERVICE
1440 South Priest Drive, Tempe, AZ 85281
Canadian address: Stratford, Ontario N5A 6W2

ANNE WEALE

all that heaven allows

Harlequin Books

TORONTO • NEW YORK • LOS ANGELES • LONDON
AMSTERDAM • PARIS • SYDNEY • HAMBURG
STOCKHOLM • ATHENS • TOKYO • MILAN

Then talk not of Inconstancy,
    False Hearts, and broken Vows;
If I by Miracle can be
This live-long Minute true to thee,
    'Tis all that Heav'n allows.

John Wilmot, Earl of Rochester

———————◆———————

Harlequin Presents first edition July 1983
ISBN 0-373-10613-0

Original hardcover edition published in 1983
by Mills & Boon Limited

CHAPTER ONE

THE great wrought iron gates, supported by pillars of stone each topped with a carved stone griffin with the head and wings of an eagle and the body of a lion, stood open in readiness for their arrival.

As the taxi passed through the opening in the high brick wall which surrounded the whole of the seven-hundred-acre estate, Diana saw that her mother was close to tears. It was an emotional experience, returning to one's place of birth after more than twenty years' absence.

Even though Diana herself had never had a settled home, she could understand her mother's love for the historic English country house where she had been born, and had grown up. And which she had missed every day of her long exile abroad.

Putting a warm young hand over one of her mother's thin ones, she gave it a sympathetic squeeze. It worried her that, for months now, her mother had suffered from shortness of breath, fits of wheezing and, although she denied it, persistent fatigue. According to Patience her symptoms indicated nothing more serious than a mild form of asthma, probably caused by the dusty atmosphere of the country where they had been living; or perhaps by an uncommon plant, Spain having an abundance of flora rarely found elsewhere in Europe.

Diana was not convinced by this self-diagnosis. She feared that her mother might have been concealing other symptoms because they had been so hard up that medical bills would have strained their meagre resources.

Now, thank God, the years of penny-pinching were over. Tomorrow, or the day after, she would insist on her mother seeing the local doctor and, if necessary, a specialist.

The change in their circumstances had come about three weeks earlier when, on the death of Diana's grandfather, her mother had inherited one of the ancient English baronies which, if there were no sons to inherit, descended to daughters.

With the title Baroness Marriott went the beautiful sixteenth-century house which, in a few moments' time, would come into view. From being too hard up to consult a Spanish small-town doctor, they were now in a position to afford the fees of a Harley Street consultant.

As the long, railinged drive through the park approached the crest of a rise, Lady Marriott leaned forward in her seat, her tired face suddenly alight.

'There . . . there it is!' she exclaimed eagerly.

For the first time Diana saw the grey walls and clustered chimneys of Mirefleur Abbey, the home of her mother's forebears for more than four hundred years and now their home—their safe haven after much trouble.

As the taxi rolled down the slope to where the great mansion sprawled in a sheltered hollow, its windows and gables reflected in the still surface of an artificial lake, she was conscious of an overwhelming sense of relief. The years of being wanderers were over. No more rented houses with lumpy beds. No more worrying about not having a work permit, or about how much longer their dilapidated banger would continue to run, and how they would manage without it.

All that was over and done with. From now on they would live in comfort and security.

It wasn't until they were crossing the bridge which spanned the lake that they noticed the sleek Aston Martin parked near the main entrance to the house.

'I wonder who that can belong to?' Lady Marriott murmured, looking puzzled.

While the taxi-driver was lifting their suitcases out of the boot, Diana took out her bill-fold and re-counted the notes in it. After paying the fare plus a tip, she and her mother would be reduced to their last five-pound note and some small change.

Not that anyone would have guessed their penury from their appearance. Lady Marriott's suit was an original Chanel, bought in Paris in the late Sixties during one of her husband's spells of affluence. Diana's pale green silk shirt-dress and matching cashmere jacket were equally old, but they didn't look it. With her golden tan, she might have been a rich man's daughter returning from a holiday at some smart resort rather than a girl who, until very recently, had earned her living cleaning foreigners' villas on the Costa Blanca.

Both women had thick fair hair. Lady Marriott's was starting to go grey. She wore it brushed back in a bun, a style chosen to save money but which also accentuated the patrician beauty of her features.

Diana was very much like her, with the same large, wide-set hazel eyes. But her chin was firmer than her mother's, and her lips more generously curved. Her hair swung in a loose shoulder-length bob with a soft fringe which brushed her dark eyebrows.

She wore eye make-up and lip-gloss, but nothing on her face except a sun-screening lotion, for she had a fine clear complexion which so far had needed only to be protected from the ravages of the Spanish sun.

While she was paying off the driver who had brought them on the final lap of their journey from Gatwick Airport in Sussex across the border into Hampshire, two people emerged from the house.

At first glance Diana saw that one was a thin, white-haired man in the formal clothes of a butler, followed by much younger man, very tall, even more sun-tanned than herself, and wearing a dark red jersey over a pink cotton shirt.

With his thick black hair, his colourful expensive clothes and, above all, his way of looking at women, he reminded her of the wealthy Italians staying at the luxurious hotel at Camogli not far from Genoa where she and her parents had spent their last holiday together.

Her intuition told her that he was the owner of the

Aston Martin and that, although still in his thirties, he was someone rich and important. But what he was doing at the Abbey she had to wait to find out while her mother was greeted by the older man.

'Miss Patience . . . my lady . . . welcome home!'

Clearly very much moved, the butler wrung her mother's hand.

Watching the naked emotion in both their faces as they saw what the long years had done to the people they remembered, Diana felt tears prick her own eyes. She blinked them back, suddenly conscious that the stranger, whoever he might be, was staring intently at her.

Resenting his scrutiny at such a moment, she pretended not to notice. But such was the power of his personality that she felt herself starting to blush; and it was of him rather than her grandfather's butler that she was most aware as her mother introduced them by saying, 'This is my daughter Diana, Ratty. She doesn't need to be told who you are. I've told her so many times about you and dear Mrs Bullard, and all the others who were here when I was a girl.'

Diana put out her hand, and a warm smile replaced the hauteur of a few seconds earlier.

'How do you do, Mr Ratclyffe. I'm very glad to meet you at last.'

'Welcome home, Miss Diana . . . welcome home.' His veined hand enfolded hers, and she felt herself included in the long-standing affection he had for her mother. In many ways, Ratclyffe had been more like a father to the young Patience than the moody, eccentric man who had eventually disowned her.

At this point they were interrupted by the taxi-driver, a burly Londoner who said, 'One of them cases feels like it's packed with gold bars. If you try to lift it'—to Ratclyffe—'you may do yourself an injury. 'Ave you got a strong lad you can call, or d'you want me to give you an 'and with it?'

'That's awfully kind of you——' Lady Marriott began.

'But unnecessary,' put in a deeper voice. 'I can handle

these ladies' luggage for them.'

The driver eyed the strong shoulders under the raspberry-coloured sweater. They were as broad as his own, and whereas he had a beer-drinker's paunch jutting over his belt, the taller man's torso had no slack flesh.

'Right you are, guv. I'll be off, then. Cheerio, ma'am. Cheerio, miss.'

'What a nice, helpful man,' said Lady Marriott, as the taxi moved off. 'I'm afraid it's books, not gold bars, which make the blue suitcase so heavy,' she explained to the stranger. 'Neither of us could bear to part with our particular favourites, even though there are books here to last several lifetimes'—waving her hand towards the house.

The man grasped the handle of the blue case and lifted it off the ground. His fingers were long rather than thick, not unduly broad at the knuckles but with sinewy wrists. He lifted the case with as little effort as Diana could raise the grip containing their overnight necessities.

Then he put it back on the gravel, saying, 'No doubt you're wondering who I am, Lady Marriott. Allow me to introduce myself. Reid Lockwood ... at your service,' he added, with a smiling inclination of his head which was almost but not quite a bow.

'How do you do, Mr Lockwood.' Patience offered him her hand. As he took it, she asked, 'How did you know who I am? You can never have seen me before. It's twenty-two years since I left here.'

'I read your father's obituaries in the serious newspapers. Naturally the sensational press, which I also see, didn't miss the chance to revive the story of your elopment. You must forgive me for intruding on your homecoming. Being in search of a large country house, and seeing your gates standing open on my roundabout route to Winchester, I obeyed an impulse to enquire if this estate was for sale—not realising whose property it was until your butler explained to me.'

'I see. Well, I'm afraid it isn't—for sale, I mean,'
replied Patience Marriott. 'At one time, as it wasn't
entailed, I was very much afraid my father might decide
to sell up in the way that the present Lord Camoys'
father put Stonor on the market some years ago.
Fortunately, although my father never forgave me for
marrying without his consent, he never went to *that*
extreme length.'

Diana was surprised that her mother should speak
with such candour to a total stranger. Perhaps she felt,
if the story of her runaway marriage had recently been
raked over by the scandal rags, there was little point in
being less than frank.

'It's a very large house for a widow with only one
daughter. Perhaps you may think about selling,' Reid
Lockwood suggested.

'No, never . . . never! Definitely not.' Lady Marriott
was vehement in her rejection of the idea. 'I've missed it
too much ever to leave here again, and I'm certain my
daughter will love it as much as I do. She and I have
lived all over the Continent, and I'm sure it won't be
very long before she seconds my opinion that nowhere
in Europe has more to offer than this lovely part of the
south of England.'

He switched his grey gaze to Diana. 'Don't you think
you're likely to miss the sun, Miss Holland? I know it's
shining at this moment, but you won't keep your tan if
you live here, except by artificial means.'

'Is that how you stay brown?' she countered.

Somehow he didn't look the type to spend time lying
on a sunbed, deliberately working up the tan which lent
his strongly marked features a somewhat Red Indian
cast.

Diana hadn't much time for men so concerned with
their appearance that they had their fingernails
manicured and their hair professionally styled. Not
that, physically, Reid Lockwood activated any of her
prejudices. Yet there was something about him which
made her wary of him.

'No, I have the best of several worlds,' was his

equable answer. 'It's my good luck to enjoy the spring and summer in this country, and the autumn and winter in warmer climates.'

With which he picked up both cases, and waited for the two women to precede him into the house.

'Which rooms have you put us in, Ratty?' asked her mother, as they entered the hall with its wide stone staircase leading up to the first floor.

'I thought you would wish to have the Blue Room, my lady, and for the time being I've put Miss Diana in the Octagon Room.'

'Oh, splendid. She's always liked the sound of the Octagon Room, and she knows where it is. She can show Mr Lockwood the way while you make some tea for us, and I sit down for a few minutes. It's ridiculous, but I suddenly feel rather limp. I suppose it's a form of reaction. Now don't start fussing over me, darling'—this as Diana made an anxious movement towards her. 'A cup of tea and a little rest, and I shall be as right as ninepence.'

'There's a fire in the library, my lady. I thought, coming from Spain, you would be bound to feel the cold for a week or two.'

'Tea by the fire—what could be nicer? Lead me to it, Ratty.' Tucking her hand through the crook of his arm, she flashed her sweet smile at the others before moving away.

For some moments Diana remained where she stood, unconvinced by her mother's light manner. She suspected that Patience had taken the old man's arm not merely as a gesture of affection but in order to steady herself, and that 'limp' was a euphemism for 'faint'.

Twice in the past couple of months she had seen her mother stagger and clutch at the furniture for support. Although she denied it, probably there had been other attacks of giddiness when Diana was out of the house; and although Patience dismissed the attacks as 'just part of middle-age, dearest', her daughter was afraid they might have a more serious cause.

Her mother had run away from the home the day after her twenty-first birthday. Diana, now almost twenty, had been born a year later. It seemed extremely unlikely that, at forty-two, with a figure even slimmer than her daughter's and a taut jaw and unwrinkled neck, Lady Marriott was justified in attributing her symptoms to the menopause. There had to be some other reason for them.

Reluctantly, unaware how clearly her face reflected her inner anxiety, she began to mount the staircase, avoiding those parts of the treads where the feet of a once bustling household had, over the centuries, worn and polished the stone until it was dangerously slippery and, for safety, needed to be patched with new stone.

'How is it that you know the way if this is your first visit to the Abbey?' asked the man who was following her upstairs.

'My mother has been describing the house to me since I was a little girl. Instead of telling me fairy stories, she told me the history of her family. Unless things have changed since she lived here, I know exactly how each room is furnished down to the smallest detail.'

Reaching the half landing, she paused to glance at him. 'What made you think it might be for sale? Surely, if it had been, there would have been a notice on the gates?'

'Not necessarily. Properties of this size don't always have a For Sale board. If they're standing empty a sign attracts vandals. If they're not, it encourages visitors who are time-wasters rather than genuine prospective buyers. The sale of a large country house is usually handled by a firm such as Knight, Frank & Rutley, who may or may not advertise it in one of the glossy magazines. I thought the place might be for sale because of the signs of neglect.'

'Signs of neglect?' Diana echoed blankly.

'Perhaps you were too excited to notice, but it's years since either the gates or the lodge—which is empty— have had a coat of paint. If you'd stopped to look over the wall of the lodge cottage garden, you would have seen weeds up to waist height. More than half the drive needs re-surfacing. Many of the trees in the park need lopping, and some need felling. The shrubberies round the lake are overgrown. To anyone looking at it critically, the whole place reeks of neglect.'

Diana did vaguely recall that, in places, the surface of the drive had crumbled, with weeds growing through the fissures, but accustomed as she was to the poor state of most minor roads and private drives in Spain, she had not seen it as a sign of dereliction.

'Perhaps out of doors, but not here,' she answered, touching the gleaming brass handrail which topped the elaborate design of the wrought iron balustrade.

Coming from a country where capricious winds and a parched, dry soil made elaborate ironwork a bane to anyone who didn't enjoy daily dusting, she had noticed at once the immaculate state of the balustrade, and the lovely smell of beeswax polish which mingled with the scent of the hyacinths in pots on the wide embrasures of the staircase windows.

'No, it's less noticeable here,' Reid Lockwood agreed. 'But that might be because the old boy has recruited a corps of cleaners to put some of the rooms in good order. According to one of the papers which sent a reporter down here to talk to the locals, Lord Marriott in his last years became almost as eccentric as the owner of Erddig, in Wales, who used to let sheep wander about his drawing-room, and sat down to dinner in gumboots because there were pools of water all over his dining-room floor.'

'My grandfather must always have been a very strange man, or he wouldn't have disowned his only child for refusing to marry someone he liked but she didn't,' said Diana.

The fact that her grandfather had been proved correct in his assessment of her mother's choice of a husband as 'an unscrupulous bounder who will lead you a dog's life' didn't mitigate the cruelty of his refusal ever to see her again.

Not that Patience had loved her father; he had not been a lovable or loving person. It had been the banishment from her beloved Abbey which had punished her so painfully. Never to see it again had been as terrible to her as excommunication to a devout Catholic.

They reached the head of the stairs. Diana turned left along the wide, well-lighted gallery which, in earlier centuries, had served as a place for the family to exercise when bad weather prevented them from walking in the grounds.

Here, according to her mother, hung some of the most important paintings in the collection of masterpieces assembled by many generations of Skeltons, this being her mother's maiden name.

Now, leading the way to the other end of the Long Gallery, Diana looked in vain for the portraits so often described to her. They were no longer there.

The bedrooms prepared for their use were in the east wing of the Abbey. The Blue Room, she knew, took its name from a seventeenth-century bed hung with faded blue Spitalfields silk, the ornate canopy surmounted by four tasselled vases of blue ostrich feathers.

Even so, knowing what she would see when she opened the door, she could not repress a small gasp of delight at the splendour of the reality.

After a moment, remembering her companion, she turned to him.

'Would you put both the cases in here, please.'

Removing his appreciative gaze from the enormous bed, he glanced round the rest of the room. 'Are there no luggage racks?'

'There don't seem to be. It doesn't matter. I can unpack from the floor.'

'You don't expect to have the unpacking done for you, I gather?'

'I don't know. I hadn't thought about it. I've always done my own unpacking. Haven't you?' she asked curiously.

'Not for some time.'

She watched him stride across the room to put the cases on their sides on the cushioned windowseat with its view, although she couldn't see it from where she was standing, of the parterre garden.

'You must be very rich,' she said bluntly, 'to be looking for a country house when you don't even live in England all the year round. What do you do, Mr Lockwood?'

He was looking out of the window, his face, with its square, jutting chin and aquiline nose, sharply profiled by the bright light of the spring afternoon. Not a face she would easily forget, even though it seemed unlikely they would meet again after this one chance encounter.

He turned. 'I'm usually referred to as a financier,' he said, studying her with the same open, unfurtive interest in her face and figure which earlier had reminded her of Italy.

'Which means,' he went on, 'that instead of working for money as most people do, I make money work for me. Today, for example, while I've been driving around the countryside, enjoying the spring weather in what your mother rightly considers to be some of the finest countryside in Europe, my money has been earning far more than I should have done had I spent the day working as a lawyer or a surgeon or whatever.'

Did he take her for a dumb blonde for whom everything had to be explained in terms a child could understand? Diana wondered, rather huffily.

Aloud, she said, 'But I believe to make money work for you, you have to have rather a lot of it in the first place. So perhaps there was a time when you did work in the conventional sense?'

'Never. My father did the hard part. He worked from the age of fourteen until he died at fifty-seven, leaving me a hundred thousand pounds. I was twenty-two at that time, and it wouldn't have been surprising if I'd squandered the lot. Fortunately I had more nous than most young men of that age, and I made up my mind that by the time I was thirty I'd be a millionaire.'

'And are you?' she added.

It was difficult to judge how old he was. There were lines on his face and a hardness about his mouth and eyes which suggested that he was an experienced man of the world who had left his youth far behind him. Yet his limber physique and thick, glossy hair were not those of most men over thirty.

The narrow military cut of his pale beige cavalry twill trousers hinted at the kind of calf and thigh muscles to be seen on the legs of the Mediterranean wind-surfers whose sport she had often longed to try had the hire of a board not been an impossible extravagance.

'Oh, yes, I've been that for some time,' he said, with a shrug. 'Now I have a much harder objective—the pursuit of happiness.'

'Aren't you happy at present?' asked Diana.

'Up to a point, but what suits a man at thirty won't do when he's forty or fifty.'

He smiled at her. When he smiled, his eyes and mouth lost their hardness. She felt the force of his charm like the warmth of a fire. But, after what had happened with Diego, charm always made her suspicious. At eighteen, innocent and trusting, she had burnt her fingers too badly ever to repeat her mistake.

'For some time I've been seeking a project to last me the rest of my life. I've had several ideas but today, here, they've suddenly crystallised. Do you know what I mean? Have you ever experienced it yourself?—The moment when vague inclinations take a definite form, and one sees the right thing to do?'

'No, I don't think I have,' she said slowly. 'For us—for my mother and me—there have never been any choices. When my father was alive, he made the decisions. Since his death, everything we've done has been dictated by the need to make ends meet. We didn't really want to live in Spain—we should have preferred to stay in France. But the cost of living was cheaper in Spain, and rents were said to be lower, so we had no option but to go there.'

It struck her, with renewed astonishment, that never before had she had such an intimate conversation with a casual acquaintance. Ten minutes ago she had not known he existed, and now they were talking about their lives as if they were friends of some duration.

Only once before, with Diego Sanchez, had she talked as freely as this as soon as this. Consequently her instincts was to withdraw behind a barrier of reserve. Yet at the same time she was curious to know why coming to the Abbey had helped this man to make up his mind about his future.

'This project you mentioned . . . how has coming here helped you?' she asked.

His hands in the pockets of his trousers, he began to stroll about the room, looking at the museum-quality furniture, and the gilt-framed oil paintings.

'I've been looking for a house as a business venture. Some time ago friends of mine bought a lease on a flat in a large manor house converted by a firm called Period and Country Properties. The place had been almost derelict before it was restored and divided into eight apartments. The object of the exercise was to save a fine house from ruin, and allow people who couldn't afford to run the whole place to enjoy a few beautiful rooms and a share of the grounds. Apparently it's not a highly profitable exercise for the restorers if they keep a high standard of workmanship, but I thought it could be made more profitable if, instead of selling long leases, the apartments were rented on a short-term basis to film people, top level businessmen and so on.'

His perambulation round the room had brought him close to where she was standing. At a little more than arm's length away, he stopped, removing his hands from his pockets and folding his arms across his broad chest. The action pulled back his shirt cuff, revealing a black-faced gold watch of unobtrusive design but wafer-thin and obviously expensive.

'Now I have a much better idea, but there isn't time to tell you about it at the moment. Your mother will be wondering where we are.'

As he said this, Ratclyffe appeared in the open doorway.

'Her ladyship asks if you would care to have tea before resuming your journey, sir.'

'That's very kind of her. I should be delighted.'

As they went downstairs to the library, Diana wondered what he had meant by 'at the moment'. When did he expect to see her again?

'Where do you live, Mr Lockwood?' she asked, as they crossed the lofty gothic hall with its huge hearth and great stone chimney-breast carved with the Skelton coat of arms—Skelton was the family name—and the family motto, *Auxilium meum ab alto*. My help comes from on high.

'I have flats in London and New York, but I don't regard either of them as my home. They are no more than *pieds-à-terre*. For an unmarried man in his twenties, a home is unnecessary. It's better to be free of all encumbrances.'

'In that case why bother with flats? Why not live in hotels?' Diana remarked.

'I never waste money,' was his answer. 'A flat is an investment. Staying in hotels is money down the drain . . . as is living in a rented house,' he added. 'You and your mother would have done better to have bought a small place.'

'How could we, without any capital?'

'Didn't your father leave you anything?'

It was on the tip of her tongue to say, 'Only debts,' but she bit the words back and shook her head.

The library was not very large. Like her grandfather, most of the Marriott's had been sporting men. Only one of them, George, the fifth Baron, had been a bibliophile. He had stocked the library in the middle of the eighteenth century, and it was still as he had left it, the close-packed rows of his books emanating the soothing smell of handmade rag paper and old leather, the gilt on the backstrips glinting in the light from the fire.

Her mother was sitting in a chair behind a low table spread with a lacy cloth and set with a tray of silver tea things, three pretty porcelain cups and saucers, various dishes of things to eat, and a kettle perched on a spirit stove.

'Dear old Ratty! He's remembered all the things I liked as a girl,' she said, as they joined her by the fire. 'Hot buttered crumpets ... brown bread and cream cheese sandwiches ... Mrs Bullard's date and walnut cake. Not made by her now, alas. She's been dead for six years. But he still has her recipe book. Sit there, Mr Lockwood. I think that's the most comfortable chair for someone of your height.'

'Thank you.' He waited for Diana to seat herself before lowering his tall frame into the large leather wing chair recommended by his hostess.

Then he said, 'If, as I gather, Mrs Bullard was Lord Marriott's cook, and she left a book of special recipes, it might be worth publishing. In spite of the plethora of cookery books already in print, new ones are always coming out. Of course if you have it in mind to open the house to the public, it might be better to publish it privately for your souvenir shop. Most visitors like to take away some sort of memento, I believe.'

Lady Marriott, who had looked rather startled when he spoke of admitting sightseers, replied, with scarcely less vehemence than she had rejected the idea of selling, 'The last thing I want is to open the Abbey to the public. It's not vast like Chatsworth or Woburn. There are no State Rooms here—they're all family rooms. We should have nowhere to retreat to.'

'Some owners of historic houses seem to enjoy mixing with their visitors.'

As Diana would have risen to take him a cup of tea and offer him a buttered crumpet, he rose and waited on her, continuing to talk as he did so.

'As I understand it,' he said, 'one of the most serious problems facing the owners of large houses is that, while there's no Value Added Tax on new building, there is on repairs to old property. However, I daresay you'd rather not think about things of that sort for the time being.'

'Quite,' said Diana, rather repressively.

As far as she was concerned, their most pressing problem was her mother's health. But even if Patience had been a fit woman, she could hardly be expected to apply her mind to the difficulties of her inheritance so soon after arrival.

If it was Mr Lockwood's intention to try to worry her mother into selling to him, he would have to be politely but firmly quashed. Not that he seemed an easily quashable person. It was a puzzle to her why her mother had asked him to stay to tea. Diana would have expected her to want to get rid of him as soon as possible. Not only the better to relax after the journey, but also to enjoy their first hours at the Abbey without the presence of an interloper.

To his credit, he did not outstay his welcome. Within half an hour of sitting down, he rose, saying, 'That was a delicious tea, Lady Marriott. Now I must be off. In case I can ever be of assistance to you, may I give you my telephone number?'

'Thank you. I hope you will call on us again if you find yourself in this area, Mr Lockwood.'

'With great pleasure. Goodbye.'

Unexpectedly, instead of shaking her hand, he raised it to his lips, a gesture which would not have surprised Diana on the Continent but which she had understood did not come easily to an Englishman.

Courtesy obliged her to see him off the premises. He did not kiss her hand but clasped it firmly in his, and held it while he said, 'Goodbye for the present, Miss Holland.'

Evidently the newspapers had referred to her mother by her married name as well as by her new title, or he would not have known Diana's surname.

'Goodbye. I hope you soon find a suitable house,' she said politely.

'Perhaps I already have.' He released her hand and climbed into the luxurious car.

He drove away slowly and smoothly, not scattering the gravel in a showy take-off. He might be the son of a self-made man—judging by the age at which his father

had left school—but there was nothing overtlay
nouveau-riche about Reid Lockwood, Diana thought,
as she watched the car glide over the bridge. Except,
perhaps, that arrogant statement—I had more nous
than most young men of that age, and I made up my
mind that by the time I was thirty I'd be a millionaire.

Walking back into the house, she considered his
parting remark. It could only be taken to mean he
expected her mother to change her mind about selling.

Diana had grown up with the belief that her
grandfather was an extremely rich man. Whereas she
herself had had almost no formal schooling, her mother
had been educated at a very expensive girls' boarding
school, followed by a year in Switzerland, followed by a
season of dances and other social events during which,
it had been hoped, she would meet a suitable husband.

She had been among the last group of débutantes t
be presented at Court before the Queen had abolishe
the presentation ceremonies as being out of keeping
with the times. For her coming out dance, Patience had
worn a breathtaking white tulle dress by Yves Saint
Laurent, still, at that time, the heir to Christian Dior
who had died a short time before.

The dress, unless Lord Marriott had got rid of it
might still be somewhere in the Abbey. But the pearls
left to her by her mother, and the diamond drop ear-
rings given to her by her father for her coming out, had
been in Patience's luggage when she ran away to France
with Denzil Holland. A few years later, when he was
deeply in debt, it had been necessary to sell them.

Thinking of their strange life with him—sometimes
cosseted with every conceivable luxury, sometimes
almost penniless—Diana heaved a deep sigh.

She had taken for granted that, once here, all their
problems would be over. Perhaps that confidence had
been ill-founded. A lot could happen in two decades,
and it might be that the estate was no longer as
prosperous as it had been.

Normally Diana was an early riser. But it was an hour

later than usual when she woke up the following morning in the eight-sided room which was part of an octagonal tower, one of many additions to the original thirteenth-century Abbey.

The room had no washing facilities. It was necessary to walk to the nearest bathroom, a large old-fashioned apartment with a curtain of green beads cross the lower part of the window, and both bath and lavatory boxed in with polished mahogany.

Before returning to the bedroom, Diana looked in on her mother and was pleased to see her still asleep.

When Ratclyffe had asked what time she wished for morning tea, Lady Marriott had said eight o'clock, which was in about ten minutes' time. Diana thought it would be better if she were not disturbed. To forestall the arrival of the tea she hurried downstairs and passed through the baize-padded door which separated the family part of the house from the servants' quarters.

She expected to find a maid in the kitchen, and perhaps the new cook who had replaced Mrs Bullard. But the only person there was the old butler.

'Is anything wrong, Miss Diana?' he asked, looking somewhat surprised at the sight of her in her dressing-gown and slippers.

'No, I only wanted to ask you not to call my mother at eight. She had a tiring day yesterday. With any luck she'll sleep for another hour if she isn't disturbed.'

He nodded. 'Her ladyship doesn't look well. I remember her looking like you, Miss Diana, and now she's so thin and frail. I would hardly have recognised her.'

'She isn't well, Ratty. I'm going to make her see a doctor. But I'm sure that just being here will do wonders for her. She's missed it terribly, you know. Not only the Abbey, but England. She was never really happy living abroad.'

'I'm not surprised,' was his answer.

His tone made her hide a smile. For her own part living abroad had not been all tribulation. There were many small things she would miss, just as her mother had always missed primroses and digestive biscuits.

'It was a sad day for us all when Miss Patience left home,' he went on. 'I think I should warn you, Miss Diana, that things here are not as they were ... not as her ladyship remembers them. In those days we had a full staff. Not as large as before the last war, but sufficient to run the place properly. They are all gone now, all but myself. Some were dismissed, some gave notice. If I may speak plainly ...' He paused, looking at her uncertainly.

'Of course! Please do, Ratty,' she urged him. 'If things are in a bad way here, I'd rather you told me than Mother. I don't want her worried at this stage.'

Ratclyffe chewed his thin lips for a minute, obviously deeply reluctant to put his thoughts into words.

'A very bad way, I'm afraid ... as bad as can be,' he said gravely. 'His Lordship was always a drinker, but after Miss Patience ran away he began to drink even more heavily. It was almost as if he wanted the place to go to rack and ruin. First he quarrelled with his land agent. A year or two later he dismissed a very good farm manager. What with trying to run things himself, and losing his temper with everyone, and being in his cups more often than he was sober, it was a wonder he lasted as long as he did. To make matters worse he lost a great deal of money on some ill-advised speculations. His lawyers tried to restrain him, as did the few friends he had. But he wouldn't listen ... he told them all to go to the devil. I don't like to say it, Miss Diana, but it's my belief the drinking deranged him. No man of sound mind would have acted as your grandfather did.'

'Did he never quarrel with you, Ratty?'

'He threatened to sack me once or twice, but changed his mind the next day.'

'Why did you stay with him? He sounds a most unpleasant person to work for.'

'I was born here, Miss Diana. My father was the head gardener in your great-grandfather's time, and my mother was Her Ladyship's personal maid. She was thought to have married beneath her, I believe. Be that

as it may, I was born in the Lodge by the West Gate, and
I've spent all my life here. I was fifty-six at the time Miss
Patience left home. Now I'm nearer to eighty than
seventy.'

'Are you really?' she exclaimed, in astonishment. He
didn't look it. She had thought he was in his late sixties.
'But you should have retired years ago. Surely my
grandfather wouldn't have refused you a pension after a
lifetime of service?'

'His Lordship stopped paying my wages when I became
eligible for the Old Age Pension,' he said dryly. 'But it
made no difference. I didn't want to retire. My work here
has never been a labour to me. I don't want to sit about
waiting for death as so many old men do. And now that
Her Ladyship has come back, it will be a pleasure to me to
serve her as long as I can. But I'm afraid she has a great
many problems awaiting her and, if she's not well, they
may be too much for her,' he added anxiously.

'They won't be too much for me,' Diana assured him
resolutely.

She would have had her breakfast in the kitchen,
sitting at one end of the long scrubbed deal kitchen
table. But the old man wouldn't hear of it, and insisted
she had it in the dining-room. Usually her breakfast
consisted of a bowl of muesli followed by fruit and
yogurt with several cups of coffee.

This morning she had grilled kippers with toast
and a thick-cut marmalade which turned out to have
been made by Ratclyffe. She discovered that, for
several years, he had been not only her grandfather's
butler and valet, but also his cook and maid of all
work.

As Reid Lockwood had surmised, he had had the
help of some local women to spruce the place up for
their arrival. Before that the only cleaning had been
what he could manage himself.

It said a great deal for his energetic constitution that the
house was still habitable, she thought. Left to most men of
his age, it would have become like a creepy castle in a
horror film—cobwebs and mildew everywhere.

When she said this to him, he replied, 'I fear a great many of the rooms *are* in that state, Miss Diana.'

'That's something I can tackle. One room a week and we'll have the place shipshape in no time. Cleaning is my speciality, and I'll do it with much more gusto in our own house than other people's.'

She explained about her job in Spain, laughing at Ratclyffe's look of horrified disapproval.

'It was the only thing I could do, Ratty, and even that was, strictly speaking, illegal. Foreigners in Spain have to have work permits, which aren't usually given for jobs which a Spaniard could do. With high unemployment, it's not an unreasonable ruling. But I had to make money somehow, so I took to illicit spring-cleaning. Even here I'd have a problem getting work. I suppose the fact that I speak three languages might help. But from what I've been told by English people, it's not enough to be able to do things—you have to have bits of paper to prove that you can. And as I had most of my schooling from Mummy—because we were never anywhere long enough to make it worthwhile to go to a proper school—those vital bits of paper are something I lack.'

Having finished her breakfast, she went up to find her mother awake and enjoying her surroundings.

'Oh, darling, isn't it lovely to be in our own home at last, not that horrid bare villa with whitewashed walls everywhere and all those terrible pictures.'

As she had grown up surrounded by a centuries-old accumulation of fine furniture, silver, paintings, marble busts and time-mellowed rugs, Lady Marriott's aesthetic sense had been constantly fretted by the garish paintings and cushion covers in the most recent of their many temporary lodgings.

'Yes, marvellous,' Diana agreed. 'What would you like for breakfast, Mummy? I think you should have it in bed today. You still look a bit tired, and if I bring you a tray it will save poor old Ratty to-ing and fro-ing from the kitchen to the dining-room. He's determined to do things in style which, when you consider the slap-happy way we've been living, is perfectly absurd.'

'Breakfast in bed would be rather nice, I must say. But I don't want anything cooked. Just a piece of toast and some coffee.'

'How about a boiled egg ... a nice brown speckled egg?' said Diana, having noticed some in the kitchen. In Spain there had been only white eggs which, although equally nutritious, were not as attractive to look at.

Half an hour later, after taking up her mother's breakfast tray and extracting a promise that she would remain where she was until lunchtime, Diana decided that, before exploring the rest of the house, she would go for a walk and pick a big bunch of the jonquils she had noticed from the taxi yesterday.

The fact that her mother had agreed to stay in bed on her first morning at home was worrying. There had been a time when Patience would have been up at first light, impatient to revisit every corner of the house and garden. Clearly the journey had taxed her more than she would admit, and no healthy person would be tired by a couple of hours on a bus, the same time in the air, followed by a forty-minute taxi ride.

Nevertheless, in spite of the nagging anxiety about what might be wrong with her mother, Diana could not help responding to the beauty of the fine spring morning and the wonderful sense of freedom which came from the knowledge that the whole of this verdant green landscape—so richly, incredibly green compared with the arid grey-brown land they had left—was theirs, their own private Eden.

In the *urbanización* where they had lived until yesterday, their peace had often been disrupted by radios playing too loudly in neighbouring gardens, and the screams of the spoilt child next door.

Here, only birdsong disturbed the timeless peace of the great park with its ancient trees and sweeping vistas, one crowned by the obelisk erected by her great-grandfather as a memorial to employees and tenants killed in the First World War, and another leading the eye

to a domed and pillared eighteenth-century summerhouse.

Before coming out Diana had changed into a pair of
well-worn white jeans and a V-necked lemon yellow
track top with a pale blue and white cotton square
knotted round her slim throat. Her shoes were Paredes,
a popular Spanish brand of training shoe which she had
found comfortable and hard-wearing everyday footwear
for the cooler months.

This outfit was much more typical of her than the
dress she had worn the day before. She liked clothes
but had very few, other than the kind of cheap, casual
separates she was wearing today.

Whenever she needed something more formal, she
borrowed from her mother's wardrobe of carefully
preserved undating classics. But except on the occasions
when they had both been invited to a drinks or dinner
party, she had not been out at night since the disaster
with Diego. He had made her distrust all Spanish men,
and although there were hundreds of foreign men living
on the Costa Blanca, they were all middle-aged and
elderly. Young men only came there on holiday. It was
very unlikely that, had she and her mother had to
remain there, she would ever have met anyone eligible.

Not that marriage was something she thought about
or looked forward to. A fulfilling career and financial
independence were more appealing and, even with her
lack of conventional education, might have been a
possibility had she been free to leave her mother and go
in search of a job as an interpreter. But how could she
have left Patience alone? It had been impossible before,
and was equally impossible now. Not that she needed a
career any more. Her life's work was here at the Abbey.

Somehow—no matter with what difficulty—she had
to redress the havoc caused by her grandfather.

Deciding to go as far as the summerhouse and back,
she broke into a leisurely run, keeping an eye out for
rabbit holes and other hazards in the rough grass.

She was pink-cheeked, and breathing fast from
running uphill, when she reched her objective. To her

surprise and confusion, she found someone there before her.

A young man was sitting on the floor, with his back against one of the pillars, eating an enormous sandwich, with a vacuum flask and a plastic cup of tea or coffee at his side.

As she stared at him in astonishment, he scrambled to his feet and swallowed the bread he had been munching. 'Good morning,' he said pleasantly. 'Lovely morning.'

Perhaps because he had several days' growth of beard, Diana had thought for a moment that he might be some kind of drop-out from whom she would do well to run a good deal faster than she had come.

But the fact that he stood up to speak to her, and had an educated voice, counterbalanced the dubious impression given by his unkempt chin.

'You must be Miss Holland,' he said. 'We heard you were coming this week. 'I'm a trespasser, I'm afraid, but old Ratclyffe knows that I come here. I'm Barney Lawrence. My father's the local doctor.'

At this, her flushed face lit up. She said eagerly, 'In that case you're a very welcome trespasser, Mr Lawrence, because I want to ask a favour of your father. You can advise me on the best time to approach him—and perhaps put in a good word for me.'

'With pleasure. But I can't believe you need to consult him professionally. I've never seen anyone who looked healthier.'

'It's not me who's not well. It's my mother. I don't know what is the matter, but I think it might be something serious. The thing is I'm not very confident I can persuade her to go to him, particularly not if it involves sitting in a waiting-room with other patients nudging and staring. I know how busy he must be, but I wondered if he could possibly spare the time to come to her. I've heard doctors don't make house calls, except to bed cases, now. Do you think your father might be prepared to make an exception in her case?'

'No problem. He'd be delighted,' his son assured her.

'It's the least he can do, considering the hours I spend in here. I'll be seeing Dad at lunch time. Maybe he can come up this afternoon. I'll come with him, if I may, and ask Lady Marriott's permission to continue working here. Then you can work the conversation round to her health. How would that be?'

'That would be marvellous,' she said gratefully. 'But I don't understand—what kind of work are you doing here?'

'I'm a wildlife artist,' he explained. 'I've been sneaking in here for years, since I was a schoolboy. For the last five years I've been drawing the changes which have taken place—particularly the way Nature has recovered her balance. Not that it was ever as badly upset inside your boundaries as it has been outside.'

A glow of excitement lit his eyes, which were light blue. His hair was only slightly darker than hers, and although he lacked her sun tan, his freckled skin was that of a man who spent more time outdoors than in. She judged him to be a year or two older than herself.

'You and your mother probably aren't aware of it yet,' he went on, 'but the Abbey estate is one of the last bastions of the English countryside as it used to be before tractors and chemical sprays began to ruin the land and kill off dozens of species which were alive at the start of this century. Have you heard of Janet Marsh?'

Diana shook her head.

'She also a natural history artist. A few years ago she published a stunning book about nature in the Itchen Valley, which is another part of Hampshire. It was *Janet Marsh's Nature Diary* which gave me the idea for my book. More recently there's been *Keith Brockie's Wildlife Sketchbook* which was drawn in Scotland. With those two books on the market, you might think there's no room for another. But mine will be rather different because of the historic house background. For instance——' He turned away to pick up a shabby portfolio. Untying the tapes, he said, 'Most of my drawings are at home, but there's one here which shows what I mean.'

He handed her a sheet of paper on which were three dated drawings of a lightly draped nymph poised on a garlanded plinth. They had been drawn from different positions and at different seasons. The third and most recent one showed the growth of gold and grey lichens on the body of the statue, and a tangle of plants which had grown up around the plinth. Both lichens and plants were shown in close-up detail on the lower part of the sheet.

'What a wonderful gift—to be able to draw like this. It's as if the lichen were growing on the paper,' Diana said sincerely.

He looked pleased. 'I'm lucky to have such a terrific subject. There's something about a forsaken garden which I hope will appeal to other people as well as to me. I shall be sorry when your mother starts putting the place to rights, as I supose is inevitable.'

'I don't know. From what Ratclyffe says, things may be too far gone. But we haven't talked to my grandfather's lawyer yet. Which reminds me, I'd better go back and organise an appointment with him. Goodbye, Mr Lawrence. I'll hope to see you again later on.'

'Why not call me Barney? What's your first name?'

'Diana.'

'If, for any reason, we can't make it this afternoon, I'll ring you up.'

'Thanks. 'Bye.'

He gave her a friendly grin. ''Bye, Diana.'

I like him, she thought, as she started to run down the incline. And she knew the reason she liked him was because he hadn't looked at her with the appraising gleam she had seen in Reid Lockwood's hard eyes. To him, and all the men like him—which included Diego Sanchez, although she had been too naïve then to recognise the signs—girls were primarily sex objects. Not people who might become friends, but playthings, potential conquests.

Perhaps Barney Lawrence hadn't looked at her in

that way because he had a steady girl, or because he didn't find her attractive. Whatever the reason, it had been a relief to meet a male whose obsession was something other than his own virility.

When she returned to the house she told her mother about him, and the beautiful drawings he had shown her.

'He wants to ask your permission to continue his work here. I suggested this afternoon. I hope that's all right, Mummy.'

'Of course. I shall be interested to meet him.'

From Ratclyffe, Diana found out the name of the long-established firm of solicitors who had been handling legal matters for the Skelton family since early in Queen Victoria's reign. Their chambers were in Winchester, an ancient city, full of history, which she was looking forward to visiting. But when she rang up, the partner to whom she was put through, young Mr Brand, suggested coming to the Abbey.

This was just as well, because later on she discovered that the only serviceable vehicle in the coach-house was Ratclyffe's bicycle. There were several cars there, including the Lanchester bought by her grandfather in 1905, but none was in roadworthy order.

'In any case I doubt if a foreign licence would be valid in England, Miss Diana,' said the butler. 'I fancy you will have to pass a test before you can drive in this country.'

'Yes, and I've never driven on the left, so I might fail it. Perhaps a better idea would be to get hold of a pony and learn to drive this trap,' she suggested, turning her attention to the first of the horse-drawn vehicles ranged alongside the motors. 'What sort of carriage is that, Ratty?'—indicating the next in line to the trap.

'That's the brougham which was used to fetch visitors from the railway station before all the branch lines were closed down,' he explained. 'The one beyond it is the Victoria in which His Lordship's grandmother used to visit the tenants' families.'

At four o'clock, for the second day in succession,

they had tea by the fire in the library, and Diana was reminded of the tall, autocratic man who had sat in the wing chair yesterday.

Today it was occupied by Doctor Lawrence, a thick-set man with grey hair who had taken over the practice from his father, and expected shortly to be partnered and eventually succeeded by his daughter.

Barney had brought a folder of drawings to show Lady Marriott, and she was as impressed as her daughter had been. Later Diana raised the subject of her mother's health and although, at first, Patience tried to deny there was anything the matter, in the end she admitted to not feeling well.

'Then why not let me give you a check?' said the doctor. 'I have my bag in the car. It won't take long and meanwhile perhaps your daughter would be kind enough to show Barney some of the very fine paintings which I believe you have here.'

'Has your father never been here before?' Diana asked, when they had left their parents together.

Barney shook his head. 'My grandfather came at least once, to attend to one of the maids who was taken ill during the night. But presumably if your grandparents had anything wrong with them, they consulted the top men in London. You might as well know—if you don't already—that your grandfather was a pretty odd fish.'

'He drank like one, by all accounts,' she said, with a grimace.

'So they say. I saw him two or three times—taking care that he didn't spot me—and he had all the hallmarks, I must say. Purple face, bleary eyes and so on. It's amazing this place has never been burgled with only two very old men here, one of them smashed as often as not. Don't you think it would be wise to have a guard dog?'

'Yes, perhaps it would be. I've always wanted a dog,' she confessed.

When they returned to the library, their elders were chatting about the changes which had taken place in the village in the past twenty years.

Neither of them referred to the doctor's examination but, as soon as he and Barney had gone, Diana asked, 'What did he think?'

'That I ought to have a couple of tests which he can't do himself. He's going to make the arrangements. He doesn't seem to think it's likely to be anything serious, so do stop worrying about me, darling. You're like an anxious mother hen, and that should be my rôle, not yours.'

'I love you,' Diana said simply. 'And I don't trust you not to neglect yourself. Daddy never looked after you properly—or only in spasms—and in Spain we had so little money. But from now on it's going to be different.'

However when, the next day, 'young' Mr Brand arrived, and explained their financial position to them, it appeared that they were going to be as hard up in England as they had been on the Costa Blanca.

A man of at least forty-five, with thinning brown hair and a solemn manner—he did not look as if he would smile much, even on festive occasions—he spent almost an hour describing the follies committed by her grandfather, and the difficulties confronting all land-owners, even those whose estates had not suffered from gross mismanagement over a long period.

Finally, he summed up his view of the situation by saying, 'However disagreeble the idea may be to you, Lady Marriott, my advice is to sell. It's a difficult decision to take when your family has lived here for so long. However, one has to be practical. Without a thriving estate to finance the very costly upkeep of the Abbey, this house is a millstone which can only drag you into debt.'

'What about the National Trust? Wouldn't they help us?' asked Diana.

The lawyer shook his head. 'There are too many historic houses in difficulties for the Trust to cope with them all. They have reached the point at which they can only accept properties which have a substantial endowment. A house such as this, severely neglected and with many of its treasures already disposed of, is too much of a liability.'

He turned back to her mother. 'Think it over, Lady Marriott. I'm sure that, upon reflection, you'll realise there's really no alternative. And, having sold, you will have ample means to buy or to build more suitable property where you and your daughter can live in comfort without this great burden of worry and responsibility.'

'He's right. I know he's right,' said Patience sadly, when he had gone. 'But to come home at last and not be able to stay here. It's . . . oh, it's unbearable!'

To Diana's distress, she saw her mother's mouth tremble and an instant later she burst into tears, something she had never done before, not even at her husband's funeral.

'Don't cry, Mummy. Please don't cry,' she murmured, putting her arms round her. 'I don't believe Mr Brand *is* right. He's taking a defeatist's line—or maybe the one which would make things easiest for him.'

She waited till her mother was calmer. Then, instead of remaining perched on the arm of Lady Marriott's chair, she went down on her knees on the rug and her troubled young hazel eyes looked up into the tear-streaked face so much like her own, except that Patience had crow's-feet where Diana's skin was smooth and taut, and two furrows engraved between her eyebrows where Diana's forehead was unlined.

'I don't want to give up my birthright without a fight,' she said earnestly. 'Somewhere there's a solution to this problem, and I'm going to find it. Only yesterday Mr Lockwood was telling me about a firm who do up large country houses and convert them into flats. Maybe that's the answer for us. We could keep the best flat for ourselves. Sharing the house would be better than selling it, wouldn't it?'

'I suppose it would,' Patience agreed. 'But does the Abbey lend itself to that kind of conversion? It's such a strange, rambling shape with all the additions which have been made to the original building.'

'That's something we'll have to find out. Oh, hell, I've forgotten the name of the firm he mentioned. Idiot that I am! I should have jotted it down.'

'Why not ring him up and ask him? He left us his telephone number. His card's in my bag in the bedroom.'

'No, no . . . I don't want to bother him. If I think about it, probably the name will come back to me.'

The next morning, Diana borrowed Ratty's bike and rode it to the village where she wanted to buy a carton of yogurt and an English plug for the electric yogurt-maker they had brought with them from Spain.

The village consisted of a long street of houses of many different periods, and a certain amount of modern development hidden behind the main thoroughfare.

There were two public houses, one of which, The Nun's Head, had originally been a coaching inn. It still had half a dozen bedrooms and, according to Doctor Lawrence, an excellent restaurant which featured in several good food guides.

Ratty had told her what kind of plug to ask for in the hardware shop next to the post-office, but evidently the man behind the counter didn't trust women's knowledge of electrical equipment. He asked her what the plug was for and, when she explained, said, 'Have you got someone to change it for you, miss?'

'No, but I know how to do it.'

'There have been ladies electrocuted, doing wiring themselves and getting it wrong,' he said lugubriously. 'If you like to bring in the lead, I'll do it for you. Won't take two minutes, and better to be safe than sorry.'

'How kind of you, but I can manage. I'm really quite handy—for a female,' Diana added demurely, conceal-ing the twinkle in her eyes.

If, as Barney had said, the Abbey estate was a bastion of Nature undisturbed, it looked as if the village was a bastion of male superiority. All the same, it was nice of him to be concerned.

He came from behind the counter to open the door for her, making the old-fashioned bell jangle on its metal spring.

'That's Mr Ratclyffe's bicycle, isn't it?' he asked, as she swung a leg over the saddle.

'Yes. I'm Diana Holland. Are you'——glancing up at his fascia board——'Mr Bolter?'

He nodded, staring intently at her. 'How are you and your mother finding things up at the Abbey?'

She guessed that whatever she said would soon be all over the village.

'We only arrived the day before yesterday. Goodbye, Mr Bolter. Thank you.'

She pedalled away to her next stop, the village supermarket.

There, nobody took any notice of her. She bought the carton of yogurt which she needed as a starter for her first batch of the home-made kind, and a carton of unsweetened orange juice.

The car park beside The Nun's Head had been empty when first she passed by. Now her eye was caught by one car there—a grey Aston Martin. Could it be *his* car? she wondered. She couldn't remember his registration number, so the number plate was no help. If it was his car, and he was inside the pub, she could ask him the name she had forgotten. Yet she found herself oddly reluctant to initiate a second encounter.

As she deliberated, sitting astride the high bicycle on the opposite side of the road, keeping her balance with a toe-hold on the edge of the kerb, a small leaded upper window in the half-timbered façade was thrown open.

Reid Lockwood leaned over the sill. 'Good morning, Diana. You've saved me a telephone call.'

'Good morning. What are you doing here?'

'I'll explain that over a drink. You can leave your bike in the car park.'

He withdrew his dark head and disappeared, leaving Diana no choice but to do as he instructed.

CHAPTER TWO

THE interior appointments of the pub were in keeping with the sixteenth-century beams and panelling. The tables and chairs in the foyer appeared to be genuine early oak pieces—or superior reproductions—and the ornaments were pewter. Red and blue Turkey carpets gave colour and comfort to the stone floors.

A glazed door, through which she could see two old men in cloth caps drinking beer, separated the public bar from the foyer. The lounge bar was through an archway. As Diana turned in that direction, Reid Lockwood came down the staircase beside the reception desk, its panelled walls hung with several large blue and white goose platters.

'I almost didn't recognise you in that outfit,' he said, eyeing the clothes she had worn the day before. 'You look about sixteen—much younger than the first time we met.'

She remembered that she was not wearing make-up. There were days when she did, and days when she didn't. It depended on her mood. But she would have if she'd known she was going to meet him.

'Come in here,' he said, taking her elbow and steering her towards a sunny area at the end of the lounge. 'What can I get you?'

'A glass of white wine, if they have it, please.'

He saw her seated before he turned back to the bar where a barman was polishing glasses.

'Good morning, sir. What would you like?'

She heard Reid say, 'A glass of white wine for my guest, and a lager for me.'

His deep voice matched his height and build. He didn't lean against the bar but stood upright, straight-backed, waiting for the drinks to be produced. He was wearing grey flannel trousers and a coat of grey herringbone tweed with ovals of suede on the elbows. When he turned, she saw that his shirt—which she hadn't taken in before—was a very fine red and white check, with a plain red wool tie. She liked the way he dressed, even if she didn't much like the man.

When he had rejoined her, and sat down, he said, 'While I was staying with my friends in Winchester, I mentioned my visit to the Abbey, and they told me about this establishment. Apparently the food is outstanding. Why don't you stay and have lunch with me?'

'Thank you, but I have to get back. My mother will worry if I don't turn up.'

'Telephone her.'

After living for some years in Spain, where few foreigners had telephones, Diana was not accustomed to the convenience of being able to ring up.

'Better still, I'll speak to her.' He rose. 'Do you know the number?'

She shook her hed.

'Doesn't matter—the receptionist will get it for me. Shan't be long.' He strode briskly away.

It wouldn't occur to him, she thought, that she might not wish to have lunch with him. She had never met a man more sure of himself, and of other people's reactions to him. But for once, in her case, he was wrong. She was not attracted to him, but to The Nun's Head's cuisine.

Like her father, she adored good food and expensive delicacies. Her mother was a brilliant cook, but she wasn't much interested in eating. Simple fare was what Patience liked best, not the caviar and truffle-flecked pâtés enjoyed by her gourmet husband whenever he had been able to afford them.

Diana sipped her chilled wine, and wondered why Reid was staying at the inn overnight when he could have had lunch and dinner there, and then driven back to his flat.

When he came back, she asked him.

'This isn't the weather for London. Tomorrow it will probably change, and then I shall go back,' he answered. 'But while this spring warmth continues I prefer to be in the country.'

She thought he was being evasive, as she had been with Mr Bolter.

After a moment, she said, 'The first time we met you spoke of a project which visiting the Abbey had crystallised, but you hadn't time to explain it to me.'

'And now I've had some fresh thoughts which I think it wiser not to discuss until they're fully formulated.'

Although he smiled as he said it, she could not help feeling put down.

She said, 'Having coerced me into having lunch with you, perhaps you could organise some cold storage for my food shopping.' She held out the plastic carrier containing the yogurt and juice.

'By all means.' He took it away, not at all put out by her request.

While he was gone, Barney walked into the bar accompanied by a girl in green dungarees and a rollneck jersey.

As Diana was the only person in the lounge, he could not fail to notice her.

'Hello, Diana. I didn't expect to see you here. Is your mother with you?' he asked approaching her chair.

'No. I'm with a . . . friend.'

'This is my sister Valentine.' He beckoned to the girl who was hovering uncertainly in his wake. 'Val, this is Diana Holland, Lady Marriott's daughter. They arrived at the Abbey the day before yesterday.'

The two girls smiled and shook hands. Diana was as drawn to Valentine as she had been to Barney and his father.

'My sister has only just arrived. She's spending the weekend at home and as lunch won't be ready for an hour we thought we'd stroll down to the Nun. What are you having, Val?'

'Lager, please, Barney. What a super tan you've got, Miss Holland. Where did you acquire it?'

'We've been living in Spain for four years.'

'Oh, really? Did you like it there?'

'In some ways. I liked the mountains and the wild

flowers. I didn't much care for the coastal fringe which has been very badly developed. You're a doctor like your father, I believe?'

'I shall be next year when I qualify.'

At this point Reid reappeared. Diana was surprised to notice that, although she was a striking girl with an excellent figure, he didn't give Valentine the head-to-foot appraisal which had put her own back up.

She introduced them, explaining who Valentine's father was. They were exchanging pleasantries when Barney joined them, a glass of lager in either hand. This time it was Valentine who performed the necessary introduction, after which Reid had little choice but to say, 'Won't you join us?'

To Diana this was not an intrusion but a relief. She didn't find Reid a relaxing person to be with.

To Valentine, she said jokingly, 'I suspect that one person who may not be too keen for you to treat him when you join your father in the practice is Mr Bolter, the ironmonger. I bought a plug from him this morning, and he was extremely dubious about my ability to fit it correctly.'

'Oh, no doubt I'll encounter quite a bit of resistance among the diehards,' said the other girl, smiling. 'But it cuts both ways. Some of the elderly women will feel more comfortable with me than they do with Father.'

'Are you also a medical student?' Reid asked her brother.

'No, an artist. By some strange quirk of genetics, I take after my mother who taught art, and Val is like Father,' he answered. 'Do I take it, from your tan, that you've also come from Spain, Mr Lockwood?' Evidently he considered that Reid was too much his senior to be addressed by his first name.

'No, mine is an Arizona tan.' Without enlarging on this statement, Reid continued to question the Lawrences about their work and ambitions.

'A nice pair. How did you meet them?' he asked, after they had gone home.

Diana was about to explain when a man whom she took to be the landlord came towards them, carrying some folders.

'Are you having lunch, Mr Lockwood?'

'We are.'

'Perhaps you'd like to look at the menu and our wine list.' He handed them to Reid, and offered a menu to Diana.

For some minutes after he had left them to study the bill of fare there was silence in their corner of the lounge. By this time there were about a dozen other people—mostly men—having pre-luncheon drinks there.

Diana was taken aback by the prices of the dishes. Spain no longer had the low cost of living which had caused them to go there four years ago, and she and her mother had never patronised the restaurants, even at the beginning of their Spanish sojourn. But she knew from other people what it cost to eat out, and it was nothing like as much as Reid was going to have to pay for their lunch here. Still, if he was really as rich as he made out, these prices wouldn't burn a hole in his pocket.

'Do you like oysters?' he asked her.

'I like everything,' she admitted.

'Good. Then let's both start with oysters followed by . . . what about the lamb cutlets?'

'If I may, I'd rather have beef. The lamb in Spain is very good but the beef isn't . . . horribly tough. I'd like to try the roast fillet of beef with mushrooms.'

'By all means. With what vegetables? It says they're all grown locally, and cooked to order which, if true, is remarkable.'

'I'd like broccoli and glazed onions, please.'

'A girl of decision—I like that. Would you care to look at the wine list, or will you leave that to me?'

'I'm sure you're far more knowledgeable than I am. My father was a connoisseur, but he couldn't often afford to drink fine wines and I was too young to share his enjoyment of them, although not too young for the wonderful meals we had sometimes.'

'You were very attached to your father?'

'No, hardly at all. I could see how selfish he was . . . how right my grandfather had been to distrust him. I suppose Father must have thought that, after a while, it would be a case of "all is forgiven". Or perhaps he was in love with my mother—at the beginning. If so, it didn't last long. By the time I was old enough to notice, he'd become the most self-centred man I've ever encountered. If it had been my mother who'd died when I was sixteen, I'm sure he'd have had no compunction about dumping me. But——'

She stopped short, again confounded by the ease with which he seemed able to elicit confidences.

'Did your mother continue to love him?'

Diana resented the question, yet knew she had herself invited it by telling him as much as she had.

Reluctantly, she said, 'Yes, she did. However many times he disillusioned her, she went on thinking him wonderful. In some ways he was, but his charm was completely superficial. I'm amazed that she couldn't see it. I could, when I was quite small.'

'And you don't intend to repeat her mistake?'

'No.'

But she already had. When Diego Sanchez had smiled at her with his black-lashed dark eyes, she had been as dazzled by his charm as her mother had been by her father's. But fortunately Diego hadn't wanted to marry her, only to seduce her and boast about it to his friends. So the pain had not been as protracted as her mother's experience of heartbreak.

The landlord returned, took Reid's order, and asked if they would like another drink.

Reid glanced enquiringly at her, and she shook her head. 'Not for me, thank you.'

'Nor for me. I think we'll move into the dining-room and get away from all these smokers who, one hopes, won't smoke there,' he remarked in a rather clipped tone, as he glanced at a group of four men who were making the air round them blue.

'Have you never smoked?' asked Diana, as they

moved away from the subjects of his displeasure.

'As a schoolboy—yes, for a time. But my father's premature death was an effective deterrent to continuing the habit. I enjoy life too much to want to risk missing my full span. You don't smoke, do you? You didn't appear to the other day.'

'No, lack of money prevented me ever starting, and now I'm past the age when people feel obliged to conform.'

In the dining-room they were shown to a table which didn't meet with Reid's approval. Without fuss he chose another. She sensed he was a man who was exceedingly exacting about every aspect of his life, but who would get what he wanted without ever raising his voice or throwing his weight about.

They had not long to wait before their oysters arrived, served in the half shell on a bed of crushed ice, with quarters of lemon, cayenne pepper and brown bread and butter.

'The last time I had these was in France on my fifteenth birthday. I think they were called Marennes,' she remarked, as she steadied the first shell.

Reid said, 'Some day, when you're in America, you must try their east coast Bluepoints. American seafood is excellent—and extraordinarily cheap compared with Europe.'

'I doubt if I shall ever go there,' said Diana. 'After twenty years without roots, my mother longs to stay put.'

'She may—but do you?' was his comment.

'Yes, I do—if it's possible. Which reminds me: what was the name of that firm you mentioned the other day? The one which converts country houses into flats.'

Instead of telling her, he said, 'Have you got that in mind for the Abbey now?'

'It's something we may have to consider,' Diana said guardedly.

He put down his fork and produced a pen and some paper on which he wrote down the name. The action drew her attention to the strength and beauty of his hands with their long, square-tipped fingers.

The one thing she had never liked about Diego—in the days when she had thought him wonderful—had been his unmasculine hands. But somehow she had closed her mind to them, which she knew now had been a mistake. It wasn't love which was blind, only infatuation.

'Thank you.' She put the piece of paper in her pocket, and continued eating the oysters and drinking their juice.

When the last of the six shells was empty, she sat back and smiled. 'Those were delicious!'

'I'm glad you enjoyed them,' Reid said pleasantly.

She decided to ask the question which had been on her mind for some time.

'You said I'd saved you a telephone call. What did you mean?'

'I was going to invite you to lunch with me.'

'But not to explain that project. So what other reason did you have?'

'The most obvious one. The desire of a man on his own to enjoy a meal in the company of an attractive girl.'

Diana met his smiling grey gaze with a level look which made him say, 'You don't believe me? Why not? Don't you think you're attractive?'

'I'm certainly not very chic at the moment,' she responded, glancing down at her clothes, which were not what she would have chosen to wear for the occasion.

'Although women themselves never seem to accept it, their power to attract has little or nothing to do with what they wear,' he said. 'Sophia Loren and Candice Bergen would be beautiful, bedworthy women whatever they wore. Anyway, I don't think you're greatly concerned about how you're dressed. Most girls would have spent at least ten minutes in the cloakroom before lunch. You didn't.'

She gave a slight shrug. 'I washed my hands before I came out, and I'm not carrying a comb or a lipstick, so there wasn't much I could do to myself.'

'Apart from which you have the true aristocrat's

indifference to other people's opinion.'

'I wouldn't say that—and I certainly *never* think of myself as an aristocrat,' she said emphatically.

'Naturally not—any more than you are constantly aware of having hazel eyes and a rather charming little mole high up on your left cheekbone,' answered Reid. 'We all take our inherent qualities for granted. It's other people who are aware of them. The man you were speaking of earlier, the one who didn't think you would be capable of changing an electric plug, isn't conscious of having a reactionary attitude to women. It's the way he is and always has been. Similarly, you and your mother are the products of a certain life-style, and it makes you behave in a certain way.'

'I don't agree,' she said firmly. 'For one thing my upbringing has been utterly different from Mummy's. If I don't worry what people think, it's because I have enough sense to know that they're probably much too preoccupied with their own affairs even to notice my defects.'

Reid waited until the next course had been served before he said, 'How has your upbringing differed from your Mother's?'

'In every way. She went to school. I didn't. She "came out". I haven't had even a modified season. She knew a whole host of other girls, and still keeps in touch with a few of them. I've never had any close friendships. Far from being in any way typical, I don't really fit into any group. Which I don't mind. I don't want to fit. I like being a loner,' she told him.

He watched her cut off a piece of the tender fillet, garnished with chopped mushrooms cooked with breadcrumbs and herbs and topped with Parmesan.

'If you didn't go to school, and have had no friends, it sounds as if your mother has been your most formative influence. Would you deny she was an aristocrat?'

Diana's taste-buds relished the succulent meat. She wished he would concentrate on his cutlets and let her eat in peace.

'That's different,' she said, after a moment. 'No, I

wouldn't deny that Mummy was—but probably for reasons other than those you have in mind.'

'For example?'

'Who was it—Cardinal Newman?—who defined a gentleman as somebody who never inflicted pain? I think my mother has the most perfect manners of anyone I've ever encountered. She would die rather than hurt someone's feelings. In a rush for the lifeboats, she would never be part of the stampede. In a siege, she would starve rather than see a child hungry. She believes that, if people are privileged, they have a responsibility to care for others who are less fortunate, and to set an example.'

Reid said, 'That's what Plato had in mind when he introduced his political theory of rule by the best. In Greek *aristos* means best, and *kratos* means power. Hence our word aristocrat. Unfortunately not everyone born with that label has lived up to your mother's ideals. But I would suspect that most of them have rubbed off on you.'

'You'd be wrong. I'm only like her in looks. My character isn't a patch on hers. I'm my father's daughter as well, you know, and although it wasn't a mésalliance in the social sense, in matters of principle he was an absolute mountebank.'

She paused to drink the wine he had chosen, a white Burgundy—she had glimpsed the name Chambertin on the label when the waiter had shown him the bottle—which was as good with the beef as it had been with the oysters.

'What about your mother?' she asked. 'You haven't mentioned her.'

'She lives in Italy where she was born and where my father met her. She went back there when I went to school. She had always disliked the English climate, and she and my father had nothing in common except, initially, a very powerful sexual attraction. Had they been of my generation, or yours, they would have lived together for six months and got each other out of their systems. But in those days, for an Italian girl with my mother's background, it was marriage or nothing. My Italian grandfather disapproved as strongly as yours did, but he didn't carry it to the extent of disowning her. Of course he was poor and my father was on the way to being rich, so the circumstances were different.'

'Did you never see her again? It seems so unlike an Italian woman to desert her son. Were you their only child?'

'Yes, and that was another bone of contention between them. She wanted more and my father didn't. She didn't desert me. It was I who went away to school and, being at odds with my father, and bored and lonely, she did the sensible thing. I used to spend half the holidays with her and half with him, and I much preferred being in Italy. After his death, she married the man she should have married in the first place.'

'Do you ever see her now?'

She pictured his mother as a village belle grown old and stout, living the simple life of Italian country people, and having as little in common with her worldly, jet-setting son as she'd had with his ambitious father.

'Yes, quite often,' said Reid. 'I'm rather fond of her. But she tends to produce pretty girls whom she wants me to marry, and her taste isn't mine.'

'Is Candice Bergen married? If not, as she's your ideal woman, why not propose to her?' Diana suggested teasingly.

'She's married now. But in any case as well as her film career, she's seriously interested in photography. I want a wife who is free to share my way of life.'

'Reasonable, I suppose, but perhaps not as easy as it used to be in this age of career-girls who don't want to surrender *their* life-styles. I think marriage is an impossible relationship. I've never met any married couple who, after the first year or two, aren't making the best of a bad job.'

Reid's attention had been on his plate. Now he glanced up, his grey eyes intent. 'So what's the alternative?'

'I don't know. Different partners for different ages, maybe. I read an article which suggested that as a solution. A husband to father one's children. Then, around thirty-five, an amicable separation and a new partner for one's middle years—which is what does happen in a good many cases already. Then perhaps a third partner for old age. It sounds a bit like musical chairs to me—too involved.'

'And you sound extraordinarily cynical for some-one of your age,' was his comment. 'Don't you want to experience Love with a capital L as most girls do?'

'A *coup de foudre*? No, I don't. I should know it wasn't going to last. It never does.'

'But at least you would have lived a little.'

Diana suspected him of teasing her. She sipped her wine, smiled, and said lightly, 'This is a silly conversation. Tell me more about America, as you obviously know it and like it.'

'Travellers' tales aren't as interesting as people's thoughts about life,' he countered. 'I want to know how you tick.'

'I can't imagine why,' she returned. 'Frankly, I can't think why you should be interested in me at all. Perhaps what really interests you is the Abbey? But it won't be coming on the market if I can help it. I don't mind admitting that things are in a bad way. Our lawyer thinks we should sell it. But I'm absolutely determined that, somehow, my mother is going to spend the rest of her life there.'

'If you're determined on it, I expect you'll succeed,' was his unruffled answer. 'I have no desire to dispossess you. I think it would be a great pity if your family's connection with the house were to be broken.'

Diana was rather nonplussed by this reply. She had been almost certain that he had it in mind to buy the Abbey. But somehow he didn't strike her as a man who would tamper with the truth, and if he said he didn't want the house she felt reasonably sure that he meant it.

'As for my interest in you—perhaps that has

something to do with your patent lack of interest in me,'
he continued dryly. 'For a variety of reasons—not all of
them flattering to my ego—I find most women more
forthcoming than you have been so far.'

'You mean people throw themselves at you because
you're very rich?'

'Yes.' For an instant his eyes were arctic, and a slight,
rather unpleasant smile twisted his well-cut mouth.

She could imagine the deliberate cruelty with which
he would reject lures from women who didn't appeal to
him; and the cynicism with which he would make the
most of his opportunities when he was attracted.

He had called her cynical for her age, and perhaps
she was. But only where love was concerned. She had a
feeling that his cynicism went much deeper, and applied
to all aspects of life. She had never met a man with such
hard eyes. The charm of his smile distracted one from it
sometimes. But when he wasn't smiling, his eyes were
as hard as steel.

She could imagine them gleaming with desire, but not
softening with tenderness. There was nothing sensitive
or vulnerable about Reid's face as there was about
Barney's. She doubted if anyone could hurt this man.
He had the air of wearing an invisible armour which
made him impervious to all life's slings and arrows.

'But don't run away with the idea that I have a chip
on my shoulder, and suspect every pretty face of hiding
a calculating mind,' he went on. 'I've been liked for
myself often enough to make me confident that I
shouldn't always get the brush-off if I were a poor
man.'

'I'm sure you wouldn't. You're very good-looking,'
she answered.

His lips twitched. The dispassionate tone in which she
had expressed the compliment seemed to amuse him.

'But, having said that, the attraction which I feel
towards you is not mutual—am I right?' he enquired.

With a forkful of broccoli half way to her mouth,
Diana checked and gave him a disconcerted glance.

'I—I think you're making fun of me.'

'Not at all. I'm entirely serious. The moment I came out of your house and saw you paying the taxi-driver, I thought you were one of the most attractive girls I had ever set eyes on,' he told her candidly.

Annoyingly, she felt herself starting to blush. She had no idea what to say. Men had been looking at her admiringly since she was fifteen or sixteen. One or two villa owners had attempted, when their wives weren't around, to flirt with her, even to fondle her. And Diego had been an ardent admirer from the beginning. But that was the limit of her experience with the male sex. She had never had anything to do with a sophisticated man of Reid's age. The last thing she had expected was that, at their second meeting, he would tell her he found her desirable. She didn't know how to handle it.

'I thought at first you were older—somewhere in your middle twenties,' he went on. 'A better age for me.'

She decided that the only way to react was to be equally blunt.

'I'm afraid that, even if I had been, I shouldn't have been prepared to have an affair with you.'

He didn't pretend that it wasn't what he'd had in mind. How could he? There was nothing else he could have meant, except that he'd heard the clap of thunder which was the French way of describing love at first sight. And Reid, she felt sure, had as little belief in romantic love as she had.

'Why not? Are you already involved?' he asked.

'No. I don't think affairs are a good idea. They may start out well, but they almost always end unhappily— especially for the girl.'

'Interesting! You think marriage is an impossible relationship. You disapprove of affairs. What does that leave?'

'As far as I'm personally concerned, it leaves all my time and energy free for putting the Abbey to rights.'

'A mammoth task, I agree. But as a young and beautiful girl you can't sublimate your emotions indefinitely. Pearls which aren't worn lose their lustre, and a woman without a lover lacks sparkle.'

'I may worry about that at thirty. Not at twenty,' was her riposte.

The waiter came to remove their plates, and Reid asked, 'Would you like a pudding?'

'I'd rather have cheese, if I may.'

'So would I,' he agreed.

The cheese trolley carried an excellent selection from which Diana chose Stilton, and he Camembert.

'I wonder if they have any Bath Oliver biscuits?' she said to him. 'They're one of Mummy's favourite things, but I've never tried them. I looked for them in the village shop this morning, but they didn't have them.'

'These are Bath Olivers, madam,' said the waiter, indicating some rather large, pale, round biscuits with indentations among the selection in the biscuit basket.

As she took two, he volunteered the information that she would probably have to go to Winchester to buy them.

Reid asked for coffee before the waiter had time to suggest it. Diana couldn't help wondering if, now she had made it clear that she wasn't interested in having an affair with him, he would bring their second encounter to a rapid close. But in fact he urged her to have a liqueur, and continued unhurriedly chatting about ordinary topics while their cups were refilled not once but twice.

It was Diana who suggested that it was time for her to leave. He came with her to where she had left Ratty's bicycle.

'You didn't padlock it, I see. I daresay in this little place there's not much danger of it being stolen. But a chain would be advisable elsewhere,' he remarked.

'Thank you very much for lunch. Goodbye,' she said, holding out her hand.

'Let's only say au revoir, shall we?' Reid's smile held a gleam of mockery. 'If the weather holds, I may extend my stay here.'

She rode home feeling curiously uneasy. Could it be that her point-blank rejection of his overture had acted as a challenge to him? Might he be planning a campaign to wear down her resistance? He had admitted that her lack of interest in him was part of the reason he was interested in her. Perhaps when he told her she was one of the most attractive girls he had ever seen—a wild exaggeration if ever she'd heard one—she should have looked pleased and excited, a sitting duck.

Her mother greeted her with the news that Dr Lawrence had made an appointment for her the following day, and Barney was going to drive her to Winchester.

'Why don't you come with us, darling? You can have a potter round while I'm having my tests,' Patience suggested.

Naturally she wanted to hear all about the lunch, and Diana strove to describe it without making her mother suspect that anything untoward had happened. She felt sure that Patience would be furious if she knew the line Reid had taken.

Because she had known that Lady Marriott would disapprove of Diego Sanchez, Diana had kept her relationship with him a secret. This had not involved her in lies or any elaborate subterfuge.

Between the hours of half past one and five—the so-called siesta hours, although few Spaniards actually slept through them—Diego had been free to flirt with Diana at the beach. Later, for greater privacy, he had persuaded her to meet him in the garden of a secluded villa which was one of the holiday houses she looked after.

Consequently her mother had no idea that she was no longer the starry-eyed ingénue she had been before Diego had made her grow up in a hurry.

It had been her own fault. She had known that she ought to take him home and introduce him to her mother. She hadn't because she had also known that Patience would receive him with her usual courtesy and later, very tactfully, point out that it might be better not to encourage him.

Which would have been excellent advice. It would

have been better to have had nothing to do with him. But he had been extraordinarily handsome, and Diana had been lonely and impressionable. She had not known then that, in the eyes of most Spanish youths, the blonde girls from the north of Europe were fair game.

Nor had she realised that, less than twenty years earlier, before tourism had come to that part of Spain, it had been a very backward area with much poverty and little education. Catering to the foreign sun-worshippers had brought prosperity and a superficial air of modernity. But a few miles inland, where most of the tourists never went, many women still dressed in black, only the men frequented the cafés and bars, and inside the perpetually shuttered houses people sat on upright chairs to watch television. It was in such a village, and in such a dark, comfortless house that Diego had lived.

But she hadn't found that out until later; and even if she had known from the outset that his father was a slaughterman and his grandmother wore a black headscarf and black carpet slippers, it would probably have made no difference. Infatuation took no account of the almost insuperable barriers between people of different backgrounds and different cultures.

Towards the end of their relationship Diego had seemed boorish and insensitive because she had expected too much of him. All the same it had been she who had been hurt, not he, and it had left scars on her spirit which she doubted would ever heal completely.

Much later that afternoon she went up to her room to change as they always did before supper, even if it was only to put on a different pair of trousers and another shirt.

Today, because in spite of the warm weather they tended to feel chilly in the evenings, she put on a pleated grey skirt bought from a Costa Blanca thrift shop stocked with wealthy foreigners' cast-offs, and an azalea-pink jersey.

As she tied an Italian silk square round her neck, she

noticed the small dark mole which Reid had called 'rather charming'. She touched it with the tip of her finger, although there was nothing to feel. It was just a flat spot of colour, placed like an eighteenth-century beauty spot on the slanting line of her cheekbone.

Suddenly she found herself wondering what it would be like to have one of Reid's long brown fingers touching her face, lightly stroking it.

She pushed the thought out of her mind, but it made her remember that she owed him a short letter of thanks for the lunch he had given her. She would write it at once, and then she could forget about him.

When Ratty had prepared the room for her, he had not neglected to put paper and envelopes in the leaves of the blotter on the writing table. The thick cream writing paper was probably many years old as it had only Mirefleur Abbey, Hampshire, and the telephone number on it. The envelopes had the family crest die-stamped on the flaps.

It took her about half an hour to compose a brief but graceful letter, because part of the time she was thinking about Sophia Loren and Candice Bergen whom Reid had cited as examples of the kind of women who appealed to him.

When she had done her duty, she sealed the envelope and took it downstairs with her to leave it on the table in the hall until either she or Ratty went to the village and could post it.

Reminded of the reason why she had gone to the village today, she gave a murmur of vexation as she realised that her yogurt and orange juice were still at The Nun's Head. It was too late to retrieve them now. She would just have to go without yogurt for breakfast for another morning.

As she was regretting her forgetfulness, a clangour rang through the hall and she realised someone was tugging the chain outside the main door.

Wondering who could be calling on them at this hour, she went to find out.

It was Reid who stood in the porch, carrying her

plastic bag and another package.

'You forgot your shopping,' he said.

'I know. I remembered it a minute before you rang the bell. I'm sorry to have put you to the trouble of bringing it to me. I could have picked it up tomorrow.'

'I looked to see what was in it, and concluded it was your breakfast. It was no trouble. It gave me a chance to see the Abbey as the sun was going down. It isn't as dramatic as Hardwick Hall, up in Derbyshire, but it looks very fine. Is your mother at home?'

'Yes, I think she's still in the library, reading. Won't you come in?'

'Just to have a quick word with her, if I may.' As he entered the hall, he added, 'You know, I think you would have been well advised to have looked through the judas before opening the door. You're very isolated here, with only the old man to call on in any emergency.'

'That's what Barney thinks. He says we should at least have a dog.'

'I agree with him, although a modern alarm system connected to the local police station would be better.'

'But would cost the earth, I imagine.'

As she spoke, Ratclyffe entered the hall by the door to the staff quarters. Evidently he had been in his shirt sleeves when the bell rang as he was buttoning his coat.

Seeing that she had already admitted the caller, he said, 'Good evening, sir. I'm sorry, Miss Diana, I'm afraid I'm getting a little slow.'

'It's all right, Ratty. I was here in the hall when Mr Lockwood rang the bell. Would you put these in the fridge, please'—handing over the carrier—'and may we have some sherry in the library?'

Leading the way there, she wondered what Reid wanted to say to her mother, and if he was hoping to be invited to supper.

Lady Marriott was sitting by the window, her book on her lap, watching the daylight gradually fading into dusk. There was something about her posture which tugged at Diana's heartstrings—an air of resignation

and frailness which one saw in very old women. Yet her
mother was young, with years of her life still ahead of
her, if whatever was wrong with her was curable.

'Mr Lockwood . . . how nice to see you again! Diana
tells me that you gave her a most splendiferous lunch.'
The warmth of Patience's smile disguised her hag-
gardness.

He said, 'I'm glad she enjoyed it. She mentioned that
you were particularly fond of Bath Olivers, and I
happened to see some this afternoon. They'll keep you
going until the village shop can order some for you.' He
put the package on the mahogany tripod table by her
chair.

'What a delightful surprise! How very kind of you.
I'll have one now, with some sherry. Do sit down.
Diana, would you tell Ratty we'd like some sherry—if
there is any. Oh, you already have.'

She began to undo the package. 'Rather strangely,
sherry isn't drunk a great deal in Spain, Mr
Lockwood—at least not by the foreign community. You
would think it would be, wouldn't you? But they seem
to prefer gin and tonic, or the local wine. One is very
rarely offered sherry, and as for these'—removing the
wrapping from two cylindrical packets of biscuits—'I
haven't had these for many years.'

Presently, when the butler had brought in a silver
tray bearing a decanter of pale dry sherry and three
trumpet-shaped glasses with air-twists in their tall
stems, Diana said to Reid, 'You made a reference to a
Hall in Derbyshire which was rather lost on me.'

'I was talking about Hardwick. There's a couplet about
it. *Hardwick Hall, more glass than wall*. When the sun
is at a certain angle, it makes the place look as if it were
going up in flames. You can see it as you're driving
along the motorway. In fact it's something of a hazard.
People stare at the house and forget they're on the M1.'

After some more conversation, Patience said, 'I would
ask you to join us for supper, Mr Lockwood, but we don't
eat much in the evening, and tonight we're having soup
and a salad. I'm sure you'll fare a great deal better than

that at The Nun's Head.'

'I'm not staying overnight after all—something has come up, and I'm on my way back to London. But I may come again before long.' He glanced at Diana and then turned back to her mother. 'This part of the country is new to me, and I find it pleasant and relaxing.'

'When you do, you must let me know. You must come and have lunch.'

Inwardly, Diana groaned. Her mother was playing into his hands. Before they knew where they were, he would be popping in and out like an old family friend, which was the last thing she wanted.. She had enough problems already without being constantly on guard against a pass by Reid Lockwood.

In the hall, when she was seeing him to the door, he noticed the envelope on the salver.

'Is that a local letter, or would you like it posted in London?'

'You could deliver it for me, if you would. It won't take you far out of your way.'

If he found her request surprising, and inconvenient, he gave no sign. 'By all means.'

Then she handed the envelope to him, and he saw his name written on it.

'What is this?'

'My bread-and-butter letter.'

At this he did raise his eyebrows. 'You're very prompt.'

After he had gone, Diana went to the kitchen to see if she could help Ratty with the preparation of their light supper.

'Her Ladyship has told me about the tests she is having tomorrow, Miss Diana. While you were out today, I found her half way up the staircase, looking very unwell. She wouldn't let me send for you or Dr Lawrence. I understand she has already consulted him. Do you think she will have to go into hospital?'

'I don't know, Ratty. It's possible. At least here we have the National Health Service to fall back on, which we didn't in Spain.'

'But except in the most urgent cases, when a delay

might be fatal, Health Service patients often have to wait a long time for a bed. And I don't think Her Ladyship would care for being in a public ward,' he said worriedly.

'I don't think she'd mind. She's a very friendly person, you know, and no doubt the treatment is just the same in the public wards as in the private ones. Anyway, it may not come to that,' Diana replied, in a bracing tone.

Privately, she was less sanguine; and if her mother did have to go into hospital, she wanted her to have, not only the best medical care, but every possible comfort, including privacy.

CHAPTER THREE

It was not the next day, but the day after, that Lady Marriott at last learned the reason for her symptoms.

Diana was with her when the consultant, to whom she had been referred by Dr Lawrence, said gravely, 'I'm sorry to tell you that you have a serious condition known as pulmonary hypertension. I'll try to explain it as simply as possible. The origins of the disease are still undergoing research, but its effect is to cause a collapse of the arteries and veins which supply oxygen to the lungs. This accounts for the shortness of breath from which you've been suffering. Because the heart has to work harder, pumping more blood in order to supply more oxygen, it becomes enlarged from overwork. Unfortunately, at present there is no medical treatment for the condition. It can only be corrected by surgery.'

Diana looked at her mother. Patience was sitting with her legs crossed, and her elbows on the arms of her chair. Her fingers were loosely linked above her lap. She looked completely composed.

'What happens without surgery?' she asked quietly.

'After a time the heart can no longer perform its function.'

'How much time?'

'That's very difficult to say. Perhaps two years ... perhaps four.'

It was Diana who drew in a sharp, anguished breath.

Her mother said calmly, 'And what are the chances of the operation being successful?'

'There again it's very hard to generalise. This is a comparatively new operation, and we can't give any long-term guarantees. But it offers a chance of leading an almost normal life whereas, without it, there is no hope of recovery. I must be plain with you, Lady Marriott. Your present symptoms will become progressively more severe. At your age, and in your circumstances, I would advise you to undergo the transplant.'

As if at a secret signal, mother and daughter reached across the space between their chairs to clasp each other's hand. It was an instinctive gesture of mutual comfort.

'I hadn't realised a transplant was involved,' said Patience.

Diana marvelled at her mother's amazing composure when she herself felt sick with apprehension.

'Yes, a transplant of both heart and lungs,' the consultant was saying.

He went on to explain in more detail what the operation involved; the surgical technique being comparatively straightforward with the patient's blood flow being maintained by a heart-lung machine while the inefficient organs were removed and replaced with healthy ones.

The complications arose from the body's tendency to reject alien organs, but now this had been overcome by the development of a new anti-rejection drug which did not interfere with the healing of the windpipe suture, and did not reduce the patient's resistance to infection as much as previous immunosuppressants.

'But I must make it clear that it will be necessary for you to take this drug for the rest of your life, and over a period of time it can have serious side effects,' he warned.

Patience said, 'You spoke of an "almost normal" life. What does that mean exactly? If I'm always going to be an invalid, I would rather let things take their course.'

'No, no—you won't be an invalid,' he answered. 'In fact you'll be able to resume a much more strenuous life than you're leading at present. But you will have to cut out certain things, such as coffee and salt, and you'll always have to be careful to avoid infection. That can be a problem for people whose lives involve daily journeys by public transport, or working in crowded stores and large offices. But in your own case, living in a large house with extensive grounds, it shouldn't be too difficult. Socially, most people are more considerate about keeping their germs to themselves when they realise that catching a cold may have more undesirable consequences for you than for themselves.'

'I see. In that case I have no choice but to accept your advice,' Patience replied, with no change in the undisturbed manner she had maintained throughout the interview. 'How soon can it be done?'

'That I can't say. First there are tests to be completed. After that it depends when suitable organs become available.'

At this, for the first time, Lady Marriott did show some emotion. An expression of horror appeared on her beautiful, drawn face. 'You mean ... my life depends on someone else's death?'

The consultant leaned forward across his desk. 'Many accidental deaths take place every day, often to young people. It's always very sad when that happens, but at least it's no longer a total waste of a life. With the consent of their families, they can contribute to the recovery of a sick person, and to the advance of medical science.'

Diana had always known that her mother had courage. Her whole life had been a show of valiance in the face of innumerable reverses. So it was typical of her that, during the next two days, she gave no sign of being afraid of the daunting operation which was her only reprieve from a terminal illness.

Her unemotional acceptance of the ordeal forced her daughter to be equally calm. Even in bed at night, Diana dared not let go her control for fear of being red-eyed next morning. She had to be as brave as Patience.

On Sunday they went to church together, sitting in the family pew and braving the curious stares of a congregation which they guessed to be much larger than usual.

Although he had been patron of the living, with the right to appoint the incumbent in charge of the parish, Diana's grandfather had not been a religious man and nor was her mother. But she felt it her duty to set an example and when, after the service, many of the older parishioners lingered in the churchyard to speak to her, although the Vicar was at hand to introduce them, she seemed to remember them all, and none would have guessed they were speaking to a very sick woman.

The following afternoon, Ratclyffe announced a visitor.

'Mr Lockwood has called to see Miss Diana, m'lady.'

'Oh, how nice. Show him in, please, Ratty.'

Diana was not sure that she shared her mother's pleasure at Reid's arrival. With all that had happened since his last visit, she had almost forgotten him. Almost.

He must have told Ratty that he would find his own way to the library. A few minutes later, without being announced, he walked in. His first glance was for Diana before he turned to her mother, shaking hands with the charming smile which always momentarily softened the hard forceful lines of his face.

'Good afternoon, Lady Marriott. How are you?'

'Very well, thank you.'

It was part of her code, which she had instilled in Diana, never to admit to anything less than perfect fitness.

'There is really nothing more tedious,' she had said, on several occasions, 'than the details of other people's ailments. With a very close woman friend—yes, one can sometimes discuss one's health problems. Otherwise . . .

not if one wants the reputation of being an amusing conversationalist.'

And Patience had always been a parent who never expounded a precept unless it was one which she practised. Watching her now, claiming to be in excellent health when in fact her very life depended on a major operation, Diana silently applauded her mother's resolute character.

'Hello, Diana.' He turned to her, hand outstretched.

The pressure of his long, strong fingers had an oddly disturbing effect on her, and her welcome was more reserved than her mother's had been.

When asked to sit down, he said, 'In a moment, thank you. First, I have a present for Diana. It's in the car, and it might be better for you to come and have a look at it there. I'm not sure that it comes in the category of acceptable presents. You must be the arbiter of that, Lady Marriott.'

'How intriguing. What can it be?' she said, with an interested smile, as she rose to lead the way to the hall.

Reid's car was parked close to the porch.

As they moved towards it, he said to Diana, 'I hope you won't hesitate to be frank if it isn't what you want. It can go back, if you don't like it.'

Although she had no idea what he might have brought her—and was reluctant to accept any kind of present from him—she assumed it would be in the boot. But instead of going to the back of the car, he opened the front passenger door. On the seat was a basket and, in it, curled on a blanket, dozing, was a fat black Labrador puppy.

Reid bent to stroke him. 'Wake up, old boy.'

The puppy blinked, lifted his head, yawned and uncurled himself. Apparently concluding that he was expected to get out, he then launched himself out of the basket, caught his hind paws on the rim of it, and fell head over heels on the gravel. Although the surprise made him yelp, he immediately picked himself up and, after a vigorous shake, looked up at them, wagging his immature spike of a tail.

'Oh ... *you darling!*' Diana exclaimed, and went down on her knees to embrace him.

'I think that answers the question of whether he's an acceptable present, Mr Lockwood,' said her mother. 'How could anyone resist him?'

Diana rose, holding the puppy, her golden cheeks rosy with pleasure, her naturally demonstrative nature no longer masked by the defensive reserve of a few moments earlier.

'Did you see how he picked himself up? Brave as a lion, aren't you, lovie?' she said to the friendly puppy. He seemed as pleased to be cuddled as she was to cuddle him.

'What's his name?' Patience asked, as her daughter set him on his feet.

'Up to now he's been known as Bertie. But Diana can call him what she likes.'

'I think Bertie suits him,' said Diana. 'Oh, do look! When he sits down all his puppy-fat sinks to the bottom. Isn't he *sweet?*'

But having sat down for a moment, Bertie changed his mind. His next act was to cock his leg and water Reid's nearside back tyre.

'I thought that would happen pretty soon after he woke up, which is why I didn't bring him into the house,' said Reid. 'He's by no means house-trained, I'm afraid, but they're such an intelligent breed that it shouldn't take long to get him organised. Obviously he's no use as a guard dog at the moment—he thinks the whole world is his friend. But he'll grow up reasonably quickly.'

'It's terribly kind of you, Reid. I adore him. He's an absolute love,' Diana said warmly.

'I'm glad you like him. I have some instructions from his breeder about his food, and what shots he's already had and will need in future. As he's been cooped up in the car for a couple of hours, it might be a good idea if we took him for a walk,' he suggested.

'Yes, that's an excellent suggestion, but I won't come with you,' said Lady Marriott. 'I have some letters to write. I'll see you at tea.'

Bertie had already begun to explore his new surroundings. He needed no urging to scamper across the rough grass with them.

'I should think as far as the obelisk and back will be far enough for him at present,' said Reid, pulling off his red jersey and slinging it over his shoulders with the sleeves looped to hold it in place.

He began to roll up his shirt sleeves, for the day was again very warm. Before lunch, Diana had spent an hour on the terrace in her bikini. She was glad that he hadn't arrived then.

Although she wasn't normally selfconscious—perhaps her bosom was too small, but on the whole her figure wasn't bad—she felt that, with most of her flesh exposed to Reid's raking scrutiny, she probably would be.

His sinewy forearms were lightly misted with the dark hair she had noticed on his wrists, but which didn't extend over his hands. Nor, when he undid another button on his shirt, the collar being already undone, was there hair at the top of his chest. The exposed skin was nut-brown and smooth.

She remembered noticing similar details about Diego, and perhaps that was why she felt uneasy with Reid—because he made her aware of him on a very physical way, as Diego had.

With Barney she didn't feel that disturbing awareness. If he were walking beside her she would be relaxed and comfortable. She wouldn't be constantly aware that he was a man and she was a girl. They would just be two people walking a dog, chatting, enjoying the sun.

But with Reid, even when she wasn't looking at him, she could see in her mind's eye the way his broad chest and back tapered to a lean, supple waist, and the long legs which, if he chose, could outdistance her in two strides.

'Do you get much exercise?' she asked, wondering how, living mainly in London, he kept himself in such good shape.

'There's a club not far from my flat where I swim every day, and I usually run round Green Park and St. James's Park before breakfast. When I can, I enjoy playing tennis and windsurfing. How about you?'

'I walk. In Spain, I used to swim in the sea and, sometimes, in other people's pools. I shall miss that here.'

'If it were cleared of weed, you could swim in the lake.'

'Yes, I hadn't thought of that. But having been used to the Mediterranean, I'm not sure that I'm sufficiently tough to swim in colder water.'

'I know I'm not,' he said dryly. 'Cold showers in hot climates are fine. But cold baths, cold lakes and cold seas are for those of sterner stuff than I'm made of.'

Galloping over the tussocks and investigating every interesting-looking hole had exerted Bertie to the point where, on reaching the obelisk, he was ready to flop down and rest, his pink tongue dangling.

Diana sat down beside him, while Reid walked round the base of the memorial reading the inscriptions.

'What a waste,' he said, when he joined her. 'Life is short enough at its best, and I suppose most of them were about your age. Younger than I am, at any rate.'

She murmured agreement. For a few minutes she had forgotten the awful cloud hanging over them. The adorable puppy and Reid's presence had, briefly, taken her mind off the anxious thoughts which filled her days and made her restless at night.

Now, as she sat looking down at the rambling old house, wondering how long her mother would enjoy her inheritance—if indeed she could really enjoy anything at present—the depression closed in again.

'What's the matter, Diana?' he asked quietly. 'I can see there's somethng on your mind.'

She turned her head away, blinking. When she tried to utter a disclaimer, her throat was too tight for her to speak. She put out her hand to stroke Bertie, who promptly rolled on to his back, inviting her to scratch his plump tummy. His expression, seen through a blur, made her give a little gasping laugh which turned into a sob.

Even then she might have been able to control herself if the man with her hadn't moved close enough to slip an arm round her shoulders.

'Is it the house which is worrying you? Has that firm turned you down?'

She shook her head, fumbling for the tissue she had thought was in the pocket of her skirt.

'I haven't been in touch with them yet.' Her voice sounded as if she had a heavy cold. The tissue didn't seem to be there.

'What is it, then?' A large unused linen handkerchief was thrust into her hand, and at the same time she was drawn closer to him.

'It's . . . my mother. She's terribly ill. She has . . . she has to have a transplant operation.'

Suddenly the accumulated anguish of three days would not be contained any longer. Her eyes brimmed and overflowed. She buried her face in his handkerchief, her slim shoulders heaving.

Reid said nothing, letting her cry. As she struggled to recover herself, she felt sure that, although he might hide it better, inwardly he must have as little patience with her tears as Diego had had, nearly two years ago.

'I'm sorry,' she said, in a muffled voice, 'I don't make a habit of doing this.'

'Don't worry about it. I can take it.' His tone unexpectedly kind. 'When did all this happen?'

Her voice unsteady, she explained, drying her eyes as she did so, Reid's arm was still round her. She felt the strangest impulse to lean her cheek against his shoulder, and close her eyes, and stay quietly there, encircled by his strength.

Instead she said, 'I'd better be getting back. We've been warned that . . . anything might happen, at any time.'

A single muscular movement had Reid on his feet, offering his hand to pull her up. There was no way she could hide her reddened eyelids and blotched cheeks from him.

'Where will your mother be operated on?' he asked.

'In London. We don't know when. That's what upsets Mummy most ... the fact that, for her to live, someone else has to die. Otherwise she's being incredibly brave about it. You've seen her. Would you have guessed?'

'No, I shouldn't. But she wasn't looking well when I first met her. You were. Now you look tired. I think you've lost weight.'

'Perhaps ... a pound or two. I haven't felt hungry.'

'Is your mother up to dining with us at The Nun's Head tonight?'

'I should think she would enjoy it,' said Diana. 'It will help to take her mind off Thursday.'

'What happens on Thursday?'

'She has to go into hospital for all kinds of preliminary tests. After that, it's a question of waiting.'

'Can she do that here, or must she be on the spot?' he asked.

'Unfortunately she has to be close to the hospital, which means finding somewhere to stay. Dr Lawrence's daughter is making enquiries about that for us. She's not at the same hospital, but she has friends in that part of London, and she thinks she can find us some reasonably priced accommodation.'

'Are your finances as straitened as that?'

Diana had forgotten she was talking to a man of, to her, unimaginable wealth. Not wanting to dwell on their difficulties when she was already suffering from the mortification of having burst into tears, she said, 'It's difficult to say at present. We may be better off than we think when the death duties have been worked out. But for the time being we feel it's best to play safe.'

It wasn't until they were dining with him that evening that Reid said, 'Diana has told me about your operation, Lady Marriott. In the circumstances, perhaps it would have been better to delay Bertie's arrival, although I imagine Ratclyffe won't mind looking after him while you and Diana are in London.'

'Oh, no, I'm sure he'll enjoy it. The puppy will be company for him,' she answered, with a glance at her daughter in which Diana read a reproof for telling him about her mother's illness.

'It happens that I'm going to America on Wednesday,' he went on. 'I shall be away for at least three weeks. Why not make use of my flat? It's central, a great deal more comfortable than any rented accommodation, and Diana won't be alone there. She'll have my housekeeper to keep an eye on her.'

'I don't need keeping an eye on,' was Diana's reaction.

Again her mother looked reproving. 'How extraordinarily kind of you to suggest it, Reid,' she said quickly.

'Not at all. I'm delighted to help. I suggest you come up tomorrow so that I can see you installed before I take off.'

'But Val Lawrence is making arrangements for us,' Diana objected.

'She's hoping to. She hasn't yet done so,' he said. 'What's the point of paying for a place when, for the time being, you can use mine?'

'But we've only just met you,' she said awkwardly.

'Are you trying to say that you have doubts about my integrity, Diana?' he enquired, with a sardonic gleam. 'Perhaps you'd like me to produce references?'

She flushed.

Her mother said, 'Diana is concerned that we shouldn't impose on you. But I feel it must have been our guardian angel who prompted you to call at the Abbey the day we arrived, Reid. I accept your offer very gladly. It will ease my mind considerably to know that Diana isn't alone in a strange city while I'm having the tests. It will give her time to get her bearings.'

'It's arranged, then. Good. Now perhaps I'd better take you home,' he said, with a glance at his watch.

Sitting in the back of his car, while her mother occupied the front passenger seat, Diana studied the back of his head and pondered the motive behind his offer. She could believe that giving her Bertie might have been a generous impulse, but not that the loan of his flat was an act of disinterested kindness. There had to be another reason.

'I think you're wrong,' said her mother, when they discussed it after Reid had returned to the village. 'All nice men have an instinct to help women who are without a man of their own to look after them.'

'Is "nice" the right word to describe him?' said Diana doubtfully. 'Barney is nice. Reid is something else. Which reminds me, I'd better ring Val and tell her we're fixed up—at least for the time being.'

Bertie spent his first night at the Abbey in a large grocery carton made cosy for him with a moth-eaten fur motoring rug and an old alarm clock with a loud tick which, according to Ratty, would stop him feeling lonely and whining.

Diana set her own alarm for an early hour, and was downstairs in time to take the pup into the garden before he made a puddle in the house. She wished she could take him to London with her. She had completely lost her heart to him.

After breakfast Reid came to take them to London. His flat was in a large modern block off St James's Street which, as Diana already knew, was the home of several famous clubs—Brook's, White's, the Carlton Club and Boodle's.

With its entrance in a quiet side street, the block was obviously quieter than flats on the main thoroughfares. It had round-the-clock porter service, and two lifts, one of which took them up to the fourth floor.

'My housekeeper, Mrs Lane, lives out in the suburbs,' said Reid. 'Some days she comes in at ten and leaves at three. If I'm entertaining she comes in after lunch and stays until seven or eight. She doesn't like to stay too late because she's nervous of travelling on the Underground. She'd prefer to live in, but she shares her house with a sister, also a widow, who is a semi-invalid. Mrs Lane is an excellent worker but inclined to talk too much if one isn't firm with her,' he added dryly.

The woman who opened the door to them was in her

middle fifties with tightly permed iron grey hair and a round, rosy face bare of make-up. She was wearing a jumper and skirt and a neat flowered pinafore, with a string of small pearls round her neck and a wide gold wedding ring which looked as if it wouldn't come off. her hands were slightly reddened and swollen; the hands of someone who did a lot of housework without gloves.

Having introduced her, Reid said, 'The flat has three bedrooms, one of which I use as a study. You're in my room, Lady Marriott. Mrs Lane will show you where it is and unpack for you, and I'll take Diana to the visitors' room. Then I'll show you both round the rest of the place.'

Handing Patience's suitcase, which wasn't heavy, to his housekeeper, he carried Diana's to her quarters.

The visitors' room had twin beds and a long built-in wardrobe extending the length of one wall. In a recess in the centre of this a counter, the wall behind it mirrored, served as a dressing-table. A thick cream wall-to-wall carpet covered the floor, and the bedcovers and curtains were of peach linen to match the paint on the walls.

Net curtains veiled the window panes, but through them Diana could see that the room was at the side of the building and not far from a neighbouring block.

'Not an exciting outlook,' he said, following her glance. 'The sitting-room, dining-room, and my room—where your mother is sleeping—have the best views.'

'All the same, it's a very nice room,' she said sincerely.

It reminded her of a bedroom in an expensive hotel, well furnished and with every convenience from a luggage rack to a bedside telephone. But somehow it lacked the homeliness and individuality of a room in a private house, although, at second glance, she noticed that the pictures were not decorators' prints, as in hotels, but good original watercolours and pen and ink drawings.

'Your bathroom is through there,' said Reid, pointing to a door in the corner of the bedroom. 'Is there anything you want to unpack immediately?'

Diana shook her head. The two things in their shared wardrobe which did deserve to be unpacked as soon as possible—a black silk chiffon dress, and an almond-green silk suit—were in her mother's suitcase.

He took her to see where Patience was sleeping, and then Diana discovered that the west front of the building overlooked Green Park, one of the many oases of fine trees and grass in central London.

'You didn't tell us you had this lovely green view, Reid,' said Lady Marriott, as he followed her daughter into his much larger bedroom.

He smiled. 'It's the reason I bought the flat.'

With a hand cupping Diana's elbow, he steered her close to the window from which she could look down at a garden belonging to the block. Between it and the park was a footpath.

'That's Queen's Walk,' he told her. 'To your right is Piccadilly, to your left Buckingham Palace and the Mall. If the weather continues hot, you can sunbathe in the garden below, although it won't be as peaceful as at home. There's always the drone of traffic in this part of London.' He turned to her mother. 'If you find it bothers you at night, you can close the windows— which are double—and turn on the air-conditioning. I've grown used to the sound of it myself, but I'm not a light sleeper in the sense of being disturbed by familiar noises.'

While he showed her mother how to operate the air-conditioning, Diana looked with interest at his bedroom. The colour-scheme was an expensive-looking mixture of camel and grey; a restful, elegant combination particularly suitable for a man's room.

Yet here again the room had a somewhat impersonal atmosphere. Or did it only seem rather stark because she was becoming accustomed to being surrounded by an agglomeration of the possessions of many generations of one family; a delightful clutter of pictures, books, boxes, mementoes, miniatures and photographs which gave every room in the Abbey ian intensely lived-in atmosphere?

Even when they had been gypsying round Europe with her father, her mother had always managed to create something of the same atmosphere in their dozens of temporary resting-places.

Patience had a flair for arranging everyday objects in a way which made them striking and interesting. Her pillar-to-post existence had taught her many tricks for making unattractive surroundings bearable. She had a collection of zip-on covers with which to camouflage other people's gaudy cushions, and a handsome old Paisley shawl to fling over a sofa or chair with hideous upholstery. And always, everywhere, flowers—not costly cut flowers from a florist, but wild flowers and leaves picked on walks and arranged in small, unusual containers to give a room her special touch.

In Spain she had discovered a yellow flower known as the gravy herb which could be dried and used all year round. A bunch of this, in a white mug, she had placed on the shelf in her bathroom to go with her yellow toothbrush and her yellow face-cloth.

So far Diana had not seen any flowers in Reid's flat and, apart from a stack of books on the nearer of the bedside tables and a small antique bronze on the far one, the room in which they were standing was noticeably lacking in reflections of its owner's personality.

The bed was an extra large double. She wondered if that was because its occupant was an extra large man who liked to sprawl, or because there were times when he didn't sleep alone. If Mrs Lane didn't live in, there would be no one but the porters to notice if a girl who came to dinner stayed for breakfast.

There were no flowers in the sitting-room either, she discovered a few minutes later. But three or four large Boston ferns provided some greenery, and a wall of books and a large collection of paintings made it cosier than the bedroom.

Looking at the rows of shiny new dust-jackets, Diana envied him his power to buy any book he wanted as soon as it was published. In Spain, once she had exhausted all the reading matter in the houses she had looked after—and some of them hadn't had any—her only other source had been a swap-shop for much-thumbed foreign paperbacks.

It seemed to her the ultimate luxury to be able, in a London shop, to pick up an armful of brand-new books, regardless of their price. She would rather be able to do that than have an unlimited dress allowance.

Leading off the sitting-room was a dining-room and, off that, a kitchen equipped with every modern gadget. Another door led back to the lobby. When they entered the sitting-room for the second time it was to remain there, drinking sherry, until Mrs Lane announced lunch.

Towards the end of the meal, Reid said, 'I hope you'll be comfortable here. If you have any difficulties, either Mrs Lane or one of the porters should be able to sort them out for you. You need have no misgivings about Diana being here on her own while you're in hospital, Lady Marriott. In the most unlikely event of anyone slipping into the building without being noticed, there's a peephole in the outer door through which she can take a look at anyone who rings the bell.'

'Oh, yes, I'm sure she'll be much safer here than at home, not to mention being extremely comfortable. To say "thank you" is totally inadequate. It's quite impossible to express how grateful we are to you, Reid.'

'Not at all. It's my pleasure,' he said lightly. 'Now I'll leave you to have some more coffee while I head for the airport. I've managed to get on an earlier flight, and Mrs Lane has packed for me.

He stood up and walked round the table to shake hands, first with her mother and then with Diana.

Presently, after they had heard him say goodbye to Mrs Lane and leave the flat, Patience came to see Diana's room, and to sit in the comfortable armchair and watch her unpack.

'What this room needs is some of our white lilac. What a pity we didn't bring a bunch with us,' she remarked, as Diana investigated the wardrobe and found that one section of it was fitted with banks of mahogany trays for underwear and jerseys. 'Why are you grinning at me darling?'

'Because I knew you'd say something like that before long.'

'I didn't mean to sound critical. It's only that, for all its comfort, the flat does lack a woman's touch. Mrs Lane obviously takes a great pride in keeping it spotless, but if Reid had a wife she would give it all the little attentions it lacks. I wonder why he isn't married? I thought he might be divorced, but apparently not. He's a bachelor.'

'He doesn't really need a wife, does he?' remarked Diana, transferring her belongings from the case to the more than adequate storage space. 'His life runs like clockwork without one. Mrs Lane caters to all his domestic needs and, as most men don't seem to be monogamous by nature anyway, he probably prefers to have a series of girl-friends.'

'You shouldn't judge all men by Daddy,' her mother said gently. 'Men are as monogamous as we are—if they find the right wife.'

It was the first time she had ever acknowledged that her husband had had a wandering eye and, on a number of occasions had stayed out all night, explaining his absence with reasons which, even in her early teens, his daughter had realised were flimsy, unconvincing pretexts.

'You were a wonderful wife,' Diana said, rather bitterly, remembering the patient forbearance with which her mother had borne all the ups and downs of life with her father.

'But not right for him. I was always secretly hankering for a settled home somewhere, and the kind of humdrum daily round which would have bored him to extinction. When we were first married, he wanted to sell the jewels I inherited from my mother and buy an ocean-going yacht to sail the world. He was an experienced helmsman, but I'd never done any sailing, and the whole idea terrified me. Also I didn't want to sell the diamonds—not that I kept them for long. Poor darling, it is a shame—they would have been yours now. Every time I see a picture of the Princess of Wales wearing her lovely jewels, I feel a pang of remorse for depriving you of yours.'

'That's silly. I don't need jewels. I don't lead that kind of life.'

'You haven't so far, but you may. Which reminds me, there was one thing I didn't take with me—the tiara. It must still be in the bank. It was one of the heavier sort, rather cumbersome, I always thought. But I expect the stones are good. Perhaps we could have them re-set into several lighter pieces.'

'I think it would be better to sell it and put the money to a more useful purpose,' said Diana.

Having finished her unpacking, she put her case and the rack on which it had rested inside one of the empty cupboards.

'Would you like to go for a gentle amble, Mummy?'

After saying goodbye to Mrs Lane, who was leaving early that day, they set out for a leisurely walk.

'Isn't the façade of Boodle's elegant?' said Patience, pausing on the other side of St James's to admire the club's famous bow window. 'But I don't care for that tower block they've erected next to it—completely out of scale in this street.'

Crossing the road into Jermyn Street, famous for its men's shirtmakers, they strolled as far as Fortnum & Mason where Lady Marriott had a nostalgic browse round the ground-floor grocery department with its splendid selection of cheeses, pâtés and game pies. From there they crossed Piccadilly to enter the Burlington Arcade with its many small shops selling cashmeres, kilts, fine china and crystal and exquisitely hand-embroidered table linens.

'Such lovely things there are to buy—if one has the money,' murmured Patience.

Her wistful tone made Diana long to be able to buy lovely presents for her. For herself she was content to look and admire without longing passionately to own the things in the windows. But she felt that her mother needed and deserved them to make up for the slow disillusionment of her marriage, and the long exile from everything else she held dear.

Even if she pulled through the operation, her hold on health would continue to be insecure, depending on a drug which could have unpleasant side effects. She was most unlikely to marry again. Aesthetic pleasures seemed to be all that was left to her.

They returned by way of Old Bond Street where Patience discovered that the Ellizabeth Arden beauty salon, with it dark red front door and uniformed doorman, where she had used to have her hair done, was no longer there.

'Actually London hasn't changed as much as I expected. It's a long time—twenty-two years. The last time I walked down this street, I didn't dream that the next time would be with my pretty grown-up daughter.' She smiled at Diana very fondly. 'Lucky me to have such a sweet one. Some mothers and daughters seem to be continually at loggerheads.'

They spent the evening watching Reid's large colour television. The following morning Diana went with her mother to the hospital where she was going to have a week of X-rays, blood tests and other necessary checks.

Mrs Lane was at the flat when Diana returned.

When it was time for her to leave, she said 'I'll see you tomorrow, then, Miss Holland. I hope you won't be too lonely, all on your own here, this evening.'

'I'll be fine, Mrs Lane.'

Nevertheless, later on, it was an odd feeling to be all by herself in Reid's flat in the heart of a city of more than eleven million people. Somehow all those millions of people made her feel much more on her own than she would have done in rural Spain.

Before she had supper she telephoned the Abbey to find out how Bertie was settling in. After a short chat with Ratty, she made herself a salad and a cheese omelette and had her supper on a tray, with the television on.

It was nearly midnight and she had just switched off the set and was thinking about going to bed, when the telephone rang. It could either be the hospital or Ratty calling her, and in both cases it must be because something was amiss. Praying the call wasn't from the hospital, she lifted the receiver.

'Hello?'

'Hold on, please. I have a call for you.'

The voice had an American accent, but even so it didn't occur to her that the call was coming from the other side of the Atlantic until she heard a familiar voice say, 'Hello, Diana. How are things going?'

'Reid!' she exclaimed.

After which, startled by the unexpectedness of hearing his deep voice as clearly as if he were in the next room, she was momentarily tongue-tied.

Perhaps he guessed that she was not accustomed to receiving calls from overseas. he said, 'I'm in my hotel, relaxing for an hour before going out. You, I imagine, are thinking about going to bed—or perhaps you already are in bed.'

'No . . . no, I'm still up. I've been watching a play.'

'Good?'

'Yes, very . . . well, I don't know really. Television is such a novelty to us that everything seems good.'

'You haven't television at the Abbey?'

'No. My grandfather wouldn't have it in the house, and Ratty prefers to read the paper in the—isn't this call costing about a pound a second? Why are you ringing?'

'To talk to you. What did you do with yourself today after you'd taken your mother to hospital?'

'I went to look at Trafalgar Square and spent about an hour in the National Gallery. What did you to today?'

'Attended a couple of meetings. Tonight I'm going to the theatre—I'll tell you about it tomorrow. Give my regards to your mother. Goodnight, Diana.'

Somewhat abruptly, he rang off, leaving her to wonder who was going with him to the theatre. Of one thing she could be certain; Reid in New York would not be like herself in London, a stranger in a strange city. Doubtlessly he had many friends and acquaintances there, including several glamorous women.

In which case it had been thoughtful of him to make a point of calling her, and promising to call again tomorrow.

She slept better than she had expected to, waking at her usual early hour and deciding to have half an hour's fresh air before breakfast.

'Good morning, Miss Holland. Going jogging?' the porter on duty asked, as she walked through the lobby.

'Good morning. No, only walking. Which is the quickest way to the park?'

'Green Park is your nearest, but St James's is nicer, I think you'll find. It has the lake and the ducks.' He gave her directions.

The fact that he knew her by name made Diana feel more as if she belonged there.

Although it was early, she was by no means the only person in the park. Two women who looked as if they might be office cleaners were on their way to work, and she passed a couple of joggers. There were also several drop-outs about, some who seemed to have spent the night on the park benches.

With one elderly man, eccentrically dressed but too clean and kempt to be a drop-out, and with an educated voice, she had a conversation. She had paused in surprise at the sight of two pelicans among the more ordinary lake birds, and he, walking in the opposite direction, stopped to tell her that pelicans were known to have lived in the park for over three hundred years, the original pair being thought to have been a diplomatic gift from Russia.

From him she learned, too, that tall, witty, amorous Charles II had swum in the lake and taken fast walks in the park, followed by his dogs and his courtiers. In the wide, tree-lined Mall, which she had crossed to enter the park, and where excited crowds had cheered another

Diana as she drove back to Buckingham Palace after her wedding, King Charles II had once played pall-mall, a game something like croquet.

In the afternoon, when she was allowed to spend an hour with her mother, she found Patience in good spirits.

'Everyone is being so nice to me, and it's very relaxing not to have to wrestle with another language,' she told her daughter. 'With my fractured Spanish, I should have had a terrible struggle to follow the questions and explanations had I gone into hospital there.'

Towards eleven o'clock that evening, Diana found herself waiting for the telephone to ring. When time passed and no call came, she was conscious of disappointment, but told herself that this was merely because of the solitary life she was leading at present.

At twelve, by which time she had decided that he wasn't going to call her tonight—either because he had forgotten or was busy—it started to ring. She found herself snatching at the receiver with a somewhat disquieting eagerness.

'You're through now, caller,' said the operator. Without preliminaries, the deeper voice said, 'Did you think I'd forgotten?'

'No, why should I?' she responded coolly. 'Oh, because it's later than last night? I hadn't noticed the time.'

'Watching TV again?'

'No, there seemed to be nothing much on. I've been in the kitchen, playing with your food processor.' This was true of the earlier part of the evening. 'Did you enjoy the play last night?'

'Very much.'

He told her about it, asked about her mother, and about how she had spent her day.

When Diana mentioned the old man in the park, he said, 'I shouldn't make a habit of talking to him. He's probably an alcoholic hoping to scrounge some money from you.'

'I saw some of those drifting about, but he wasn't one

of them. he had very clean ears and nails, and was well dressed in an old-fashioned way. He was wearing tweed knickerbockers with thick woollen stockings.'

'Okay, chat to him in the park, but don't ask him home to tea.'

'Naturally not! I shouldn't dream of inviting anyone here. I'm twenty, you know, not fifteen.'

'But you've led a very sheltered life. I imagine this is the first time you've been separated from your mother at night.'

'Yes, it is, but that doesn't mean I'm not fit to be let loose on my own.'

'It means you're good deal more innocent than most girls of your age,' he said dryly. Then, suddenly switching to Spanish, which she had not known he could speak, he astonished her by saying, 'Sleep well, little virgin. Goodnight.'

As Diana replaced the receiver, she could feel by the warmth of her cheeks that, even from thousands of miles away, he was capable of making her blush.

Presently, while she was undressing, she found herself remembering Diego who, far from thinking her a virgin, had assumed she was as experienced as the other northern girls he had known.

They had both been wrong, he and Reid.

The next morning Diana had her second encounter with the old man, and he told her some more about the park; how, before and throughout the long reign of Queen Victoria, there had been milk for sale from the cows which grazed there.

Diana had brought some bread, and he stayed to watch her feed the ducks and the various types of geese, as well as the jaunty London pigeons and sparrows which zoomed in from every side if anyone so much as rustled a paper bag.

Mindful of Reid's warning, she was more reserved than she might have been. When he was smoothing his moustache, which reminded her of the end of a mermaid's tail, she noticed that he wore a gold signet ring on the little finger of his left hand, and it seemed to be engraved with a small crest. He smelled faintly of some pleasant cologne, and his boots looked as if they might have been hand-made.

That night Reid did not ring up, and she couldn't deny her disappointment. She stayed awake, reading in bed, until after midnight, but the telephone remained silent.

On her third morning in London, she arrived at the park later than usual and saw no sign of the old man. But, as she was on her way back, she heard a halloo from behind her and turned to see him marching briskly towards her.

He was wearing a tweed peaked cap of the kind she had seen in photographs of Edwardian shooting parties in an album which her mother had unearthed in the library.

As he drew near, he raised it, saying, 'Good morning, young woman. If you're going in my direction, I'll show you where the last duel in London was fought.'

'I'm going up St James's towards Piccadilly.'

'So am I.' Taking her interest for granted, he set off again.

Being by now convinced of his total respectability, Diana walked with him and was shown tiny Pickering Place, an historic spot she would not have discovered on her own.

When they had emerged from the narrow passage which led to it, the old man again raised his cap and said goodbye and stumped off. A few minutes later, glancing over her shoulder, she saw him go into one of the clubs where, as he seemed too old to be a club servant, she concluded he must be a member.

So much for Reid's awful warnings! she thought, with a grin.

For the second night in succession, there was no call from America. Reid's next call came in the morning, while she was brushing her teeth.

'But surely it's the middle of the night where you are?' she said, in amazement.

'I've been to a party. It's still going on, as a matter of fact, but I want to snatch a few hours' sleep before catching a plane to the west coast. I probably won't ring you again until I come back to New York at the end of the week. Is everything all right? No problems?'

'Everything's fine, thank you. Have a good trip.'

'Thanks. Goodbye.'

They had only talked for a few moments, but she went back to finish her teeth feeling pleased that Reid hadn't forgotten her, and sorry that she couldn't expect to hear from him again for at least ten days.

During that time her mother came out of hospital and began the difficult period of waiting for the healthy organs which would give her a new lease of life. The nervous suspense of this interval made it difficult for Patience to concentrate on books borrowed from Harrods' lending library. Mrs Lane suggested that some knitting might help to occupy her, but Diana had a better idea.

The Abbey was full of needlework done by the women of the family over many centuries, ranging from the seventeenth-century crewelwork hangings for a four-poster bed to the Berlin woolwork pictures of Victorian times.

It seemed to her that, rather than knitting a garment which inevitably would have a short life, her mother would derive more satisfaction from a piece of embroidery which would last as long as those of her ancestresses. She would feel she was contributing something to the history of the house, and leaving a reminder of her place in it.

To find something suitable was not, however, as easy as it had seemed when she had thought of the idea. In her opinion, a great many modern embroideries were either hideous or out of keeping with a setting such as the Abbey.

Mrs Lane had another suggestion. 'What about a Royal Wedding sampler, Miss Holland, if there are still some about? I should try the Royal School of Needlework. I used to work for a lady who bought all her wools there.'

So the following morning Diana walked to the Royal School where, to her delight, they still had a few of the samplers which had been designed to commemorate the wedding of the Prince and Princess of Wales.

'Her grandfather, the seventh Lord Spencer, used to be our chairman,' she was told by the member of the staff who wrapped the sampler for her. 'He did embroidery himself. In fact he worked six chair covers which are on show at Althrop, the family house.'

As she walked back by way of Hyde Park, the parcel in her tote bag, Diana hoped with all her heart that it might not be long before the sampler—'worked by the present Lady Marriott'—was on show at the Abbey. For the more she thought about it, the more she was convinced that opening the house to the public was the best solution to their difficulties.

To her relief, because it had been quite expensive, her mother seemed delighted with the sampler, and began work immediately. Indeed, on the following few days, it became a kind of compulsion with her. She took it up after breakfast and, except at mealtimes and during her afternoon stroll, continued to stitch until bedtime.

Another distraction for her which Diana had in mind was to ask Mr St James, as she had dubbed him, to have tea with them. She felt sure that Patience would like him, and she sensed that the old man was lonely. He never volunteered any personal information, nor did she. They were still acquaintances merely, and yet she felt that he looked forward to their daily chats.

One morning, instead of conversing on foot, he suggested sitting on a bench. She thought he looked rather unwell. They had left the park together, and were passing St James's Palace, when he staggered and collapsed.

There was no one about. Forcing down panic, Diana knelt beside him and went through the drill she had learned at a CPR day-school in Spain. She knew that, if she kept her head, soon somebody would see the prostrate figure and fetch professional help.

This was what, eventually, happened. But not until she had spent interminable minutes giving him cardiac massage and mouth-to-mouth resuscitation.

Presently, when an ambulance had arrived, and a policeman, she was asked for details which she couldn't supply. The only thing she knew was which club the old man belonged to.

But for worrying her mother if she failed to return at the expected time, Diana would have accompanied Mr St James, as she thought of him, to hospital. As it was, she could only watch the ambulance speed on its way, and hope that he would recover. The incident had shaken her, and he was on her mind for the rest of the day, although she did not tell Patience what had happened.

That night Reid rang up again. But it was her mother who, sitting beside the sitting-room telephone, answered the call and talked to him.

'Diana is very well, thank you,' she said, at one point.

Then, looking across the room at her daughter, she mouthed, 'Do you want to speak to him?'

Diana shook her head. Unless Reid asked to speak to her, she saw no reason to show a desire to talk to him.

Her concern over Mr St James led her to ring up his club and enquire about him. But the fact that she didn't know his real name seemed to inspire suspicion in whoever was on the other end of the line. She was asked to leave her name and number while enquiries were made.

This she preferred not to do. She was making the call from a telephone box. If they rang the flat while she was out, her mother would learn about Mr St James's heart attack or stroke. She did not want Patience involved in anyone else's illness; she already had enough to contend with.

'My name is Diana Holland. I'm not on the telephone. I'll ring you again tomorrow,' she said.

However, as it turned out, she did not have to make a

second call. Next morning, while she was feeding the birds and trying to make sure that a lame pigeon got his fair share, a voice said, 'Are you Miss Holland?'

She turned. A few feet behind her stood a man she had never seen in the park before; a man with greying brown hair, dressed in country tweeds and with a countryman's ruddy complexion.

'Yes, I am.' She looked enquiringly at him.

'I'm Christopher Tarrant. I believe it was your presence of mind which helped my father to survive a coronary a few days ago.'

'Is he all right? I'm so glad. He's such a delightful old man. I've been longing to know if he recovered, but his club wouldn't say.'

'He's still in the intensive care unit but, thanks to you, he has a good chance,' said his son.

'I didn't do much,' said Diana. 'The ambulance came very quickly.'

'But you held the fort during those first vital minutes, and we're very much in your debt. Thank you.' He came closer and held out his hand.

As they shook hands, he went on, 'You remind me so much of a girl I knew years ago that I think you must be the daughter of Patience Holland, whom I knew as Patience Marriott?'

'Yes, I am,' she said, taken aback.

'I read that her father had died and that she had inherited the Abbey. But you're not living there, I gather?'

'Not at present. My mother isn't very well, and she's waiting to have an operation at one of the London teaching hospitals. Would you like to come and see her? Not now, but later today?'

'I should like nothing more,' he said readily. 'What time do you suggest?'

Patience, when she heard about this encounter, said, 'Chris Tarrant . . . yes, I remember him well. Very thin and extremely shy.'

'He isn't thin now . . . rather burly. And he didn't seem shy,' said Diana.

She was not present at their reunion, having arranged to meet Val Lawrence for tea. The other girl had had problems finding somewhere for them to move when Reid came back and, so far, Diana's own enquiries had not met with success.

It was a bad time of year, the beginning of the tourist season. Apartments were either expensive or drab and depressing. Diana didn't mind for herself, but she didn't want her mother to have to put up with dismal surroundings, especially after being where they were.

However, when next he rang up, Reid told her not to worry about finding somewhere else to go as it was likely he would be away for longer than he had foreseen.

In a way this was good news. Yet she was conscious of a slight sense of disappointment that it would be some time before she saw him again.

About ten days later she was walking along Davies Street when, at the junction with Brook Street where she had to wait for the traffic lights to change, she found herself within a few yards of the entrance to Claridge's, the hotel where, having no town house, her grandparents had stayed whenever they were in London.

Her mother's coming out dance had been held at the Abbey. But several of her friends had had theirs at Claridge's, and Patience had often danced there with Denzil Holland and the other young men about town known as debs' delights.

As Diana looked towards the entrance, a silk-hatted doorman opened the door of a gleaming pale grey Rolls-Royce and offered his arm to a queenly-looking elderly woman who placed her gloved hand briefly on it as she alighted. It was entirely possible that she was a princess or arch-duchess; the hotel had many foreign royalties among its habitués.

The lights changed. The traffic coming from the direction of Grosvenor Square stopped, and Diana stepped into the roadway. As she did so, two men sprang out of a taxi which had pulled in close to the kerb outside the hotel's side entrance in the street directly ahead of her.

At the sight of the taller man, now stooping to ask the driver what the fare was, her hazel eyes widened in astonishment. It was Reid—or, if not, his double.

When she reached the opposite pavement, her way was blocked for some moments by the lead of a dog which had stopped to sniff the railings.

'Come *on*, Eggy,' his owner said impatiently, tugging the lead.

The slight delay was enough to give the man time to hand a note to the cabby and turn to enter the building. He was out of sight before Diana was close enough to call his name.

Was it Reid? How could it be, when only last night he had talked to her from New York?

Outside Claridge's side door, she peered at the two receding figures, debating whether to follow them. It wasn't as if Reid was an average-looking man. In the unlikely event of his ever being the suspect in an identification parade, the police would have a hard time finding nine other men of his height and striking appearance.

Finally, impelled by a curiosity which she knew would plague her all day if she didn't satisfy it, she followed them into the hotel, and along the corridor which connected with the spacious main hall.

Off this was a large ante-room where people met and had drinks. Diana paused on the threshold and, looking round, saw the two men in the act of seating themselves at a table in the far corner.

Reid—if it were he, but she still didn't see how it could be—had his back to her. She couldn't see his face, only his thick black hair, curling slightly where it touched the collar of his shirt, and a pair of very broad shoulders clad in a well-cut coat of lightweight grey flannel.

A waiter approached. 'Good morning, madam.'

'Good morning.' On impulse, Diana added, 'I'm meeting Mr Lockwood.

It wouldn't have surprised her if the waiter had never heard of Mr Lockwood, although, in a hotel such as this, she would expect him to conceal his ignorance by saying, 'I'm not sure that Mr Lockwood has arrived yet' and leaving it to her to point him out.

But in fact what he did say was, 'Mr Lockwood has just arrived, madam. This way, please.' And he led her to the corner table.

As she came within earshot, she heard Reid's companion, speaking Italian, say, 'And how is the beautiful Clementina? Or am I out of date, and she has been superseded by a new model?'

Reid's answer to this sally was lost in an outburst of music. On the other side of the ante-room, a small orchestra had begun to play a song by Ivor Novello.

At the same moment the man with Reid realised that Diana was being brought to their table. As he stood up, he said—and perhaps it was seeing his lip movements which enabled her to hear him—'Yes, I see that she has. But isn't this beautiful creature a little young for you, my friend?'

Reid glanced swiftly over his shoulder before he, too, rose to his feet.

'Diana!' he said, frowning at her. 'What are you doing here?'

CHAPTER FOUR

It was clear that he wasn't pleased to see her.

She said, 'I—I saw you outside, and I couldn't believe my eyes. I thought you weren't coming back for some time?'

'I ... had a sudden change of plan,' was his rather brusque reply.

'You didn't say so last night when you called from New York.' How did you get here so quickly?'

'How indeed?' the Italian murmured dryly, in his own

language. Then, in excellent English, 'Must I present myself, Reid?'

'This is Sandro Oneto, a friend of mine from Italy . . . Miss Diana Holland.'

'Miss Holland, I am delighted to meet you.' The Italian bowed over her hand. He was older than Reid, about forty-five, with a lot of grey in his hair and a deeply lined, humorous face.

'How do you do?' Diana returned his smile rather uncertainly, conscious that Reid was still frowning. 'No, thank you, I'm not going to stay'—this as he moved a chair, evidently expecting her to join them. 'I only came in to make sure that my eyes hadn't deceived me.'

'But surely, even if you can't give us the pleasure of having lunch with us, you have time for a drink,' he protested. 'Yes yes . . . I insist. We have ordered champagne, but perhaps you would prefer something else?'

'No, I'll have whatever you're having . . . but I won't stay more than five minutes,' she added, speaking to Reid. 'I'm sorry to have butted in like this, but it was so unexpected seeing you when I thought you were still in America.'

The champagne arrived. It was shown to the older man, indicating that he, not Reid, was the host. This served to increase her chagrin. Her cheeks became hot with embarrassment.

Suddenly Reid's expression altered. He said, in a more relaxed tone, 'The fact is you've caught me out in a small deception, Diana. I was *not* in New York when I called you. You merely assumed that. In fact I was here in London.'

'You were here? Why didn't you say so?'

'Because I didn't want you to start fussing about vacating the flat,' was his answer. 'Which is what you are going to do, isn't it?'—with a quizzical smile.

'But we can't stay there now that you're back. Where did you spend last night?'

'I assure you I was perfectly comfortable. It's extremely unfortunate that you happened to see us coming in here. Nevertheless I must insist that you go on making use of the flat for as long as it's necessary.'

'But we can't . . . not possibly, Reid!' She glanced at the listening Italian, who was wearing a puzzled expression.

'My mother is waiting to have a rather serious operation,' she explained. 'To give us greater privacy and comfort than we should have had in a hotel, 'Reid very kindly offered us his flat while he was on his trip to America.'

'I see. I'm sorry to hear that your mother is ill, Miss Holland. Do I take it that you are a visitor to England? You are not as pale as most English people at this time of year.'

'I still have some tan left over from living in Spain. We moved to England a short time ago. Now I really must go and leave you in peace,' she said, rising. 'Reid, please come back to the flat later. We shall move out anyway, I assure you. I know Mummy wouldn't dream of staying when she knows you're back in this country.'

'Don't rush off, Diana.' He reached out an arm, took her by the elbow, and gently but firmly forced her to sit down again. 'I'll come back to the flat, if you insist, but meanwhile drink your champagne and entertain Sandro while I make a telephone call.'

'Have you known Reid for long?' Sandro asked her, when they were alone.

'No, not long at all. He's been amazingly kind on the strength of a very short acquaintance. Have you known him long, Signor Oneto?'

'Yes, for many years . . . since he first came to Italy. Have you visited my country?'

'Only the Italian Riviera. What part of Italy do you come from?'

'From Tuscany, where many foreigners have settled because it's so beautiful. Have you moved to this country permanently, or only in order for your mother to have the operation here?'

Briefly, Diana explained their circumstances.

'What brings you to England?' she asked.

'I have business interests over here, and also I come for pleasure. My English is sufficiently good for me to enjoy the theatre—even the English jokes—and I like to go round the galleries and perhaps buy a picture or two.'

'Does your wife come with you?'

'Unfortunately I am a widower. My wife died five years ago, and my daughter is still at school, too young to come with me. When she does, I've no doubt she will be even more extravagant than her mother and I shall have no money to spare for buying pictures,' he said jokingly.

But Diana fancied she had seen in his eyes a fleeting glimpse of a grief which time had not healed completely.

When Reid came back, he said, 'History repeats itself. I've just been asking your mother if I may persuade you to have lunch with us.'

'Oh, but surely you and Signor Oneto have business matters to discuss?' she protested.

'No. What made you think that? We're merely friends. Sandro's family and my mother's family are near neighbours,' he answered.

From time to time during lunch, Diana found herself pondering the Italian's remark a few seconds before she had intruded on them.

Who was the beautiful Clementina? Was she Reid's current girl-friend, and had he spent last night with her? Was that why it didn't inconvenience him to surrender his flat to them for a while? Because he had her flat to fall back on?

However, what preoccupied her even more was where to transfer her mother. Perhaps the social worker at the hospital would be able to advise them about finding some inexpensive lodgings—if such things existed in London. It would be a wrench to leave the flat, so central, so extremely comfortable. But it had to be done. There was a definite limit to the help they could accept from someone who was still almost a stranger.

If the two men noticed her moments of inattention,

they made no remark. Their conversation ranged over a variety of subjects. Diana contributed an occasional remark, but for the most part was silent, thinking her own thoughts or listening quietly to them.

Once or twice she looked up from her plate to find Sandro eyeing her reflectively. She wondered what he was thinking.

They parted from him outside the Brook Street entrance where he was about to step into a taxi. Having kissed her hand and said goodbye, he turned to shake hands with Reid.

As he did so, he said, in rapid Italian. 'I hope you don't mean to add her to your list. She's too young, and also too nice. You could hurt this little girl if you treat her like the others, my friend.'

'Let's walk, shall we?' Reid suggested, when the taxi had drawn away.

It was less than ten minutes' walk from Claridge's to his flat. He did not say much on the way, and Diana had come to the conclusion that it was better not to resume the argument about their staying there.

She would leave it to her mother to insist that they moved elsewhere. He would not argue with Patience.

'Where had you been this morning which brought you past the hotel as we were arriving there?' he enquired, as they neared the flat.

'I'd been looking round the stores in Oxford Street. Mummy insists I go out for at least half the day, and mostly I visit museums. But today, for a change, I went shopping.'

'But you didn't buy anything?'

'There was nothing I needed.'

'It's news to me that women have to need something to buy it. In my observation, most of them have more clothes than they could wear in a lifetime,' he said dryly.

He hadn't any sisters. The only way he could speak so authoritatively was because he had known many women well enough to see the contents of their wardrobes. Clearly—as indeed she had long suspected—

he was one of those men whose attitude to women was that of the big game hunters towards animals. But nowadays civilised men didn't go on safari with a gun. They took a camera, and returned with photographs, not trophies. And they didn't treat women as playthings but as people.

'I can't afford to be extravagant,' she said shortly. And then wished she hadn't, because she didn't want to emphasise their financial difficulties.

In the entrance to the flats, the porter said, 'Good afternoon, Mr Lockwood. Had a good trip, sir?'

'Hello, Morris. How's the knee?'

'Oh, much better now, thank you sir. Don't tell me they've misrouted your luggage again?'

'No, no. I'm not coming back here just yet.'

Diana made no comment on this statement as they entered the lift and were carried upwards.

'No need to hunt for your key. Here's mine,' Reid remarked, producing it.

'Is it also your observation that most women take ages to find their latch keys?' she asked.

He looked down at her, smiling faintly. 'Are you the exception whose bag is always in order?'

'Not always,' she conceded. 'Most of the time. But a lot of the things which other people have to carry—season tickets, credit cards and so on—I've never needed.'

In the flat they found Lady Marriott and Mrs Lane sitting together, the former at work on her embroidery and the latter busily knitting.

'You're back sooner than you expected, Mr Lockwood,' said his housekeeper, putting her needles together and stabbing them through the ball of wool.

'Yes, but only passing through. I'm en route to France. Good afternoon, Lady Marriott. How are you?'

'I'm very well, thank you, Reid. Mrs Lane has made us so comfortable, and your lovely view over the park has been a constant pleasure to me.'

Her smile and her cheerful tone were those of a woman with nothing more serious on her mind than the completion of her needlework. No one would ever have guessed the tremendous ordeal she was facing with such shining courage, her daughter thought with loving pride.

'I'm glad to hear it. It's not as fine as your view, but it's a pleasant outlook for the centre of a city,' he agreed.

'Would you like a cup of tea, sir?' asked the housekeeper.

'Diana will make it, Mrs Lane,' said Patience. 'You go home before the tube gets too crowded.'

'Yes, I'll make some tea,' Diana agreed. As soon as Mrs Lane had left the room, she turned to Reid. 'I don't think you're really en route to France. You just made that up as a reason for us to stay here. Mother, Reid was in England last night, but he didn't come home because of our being here.'

'Oh, but that won't do at all,' her mother exclaimed. 'We must move out at once. That is carrying your kindness *too* far!'

Reid sat down beside her on the sofa. 'Lady Marriott, I'm catching an early flight to Paris, and I don't know how long I'm going to be on the Continent. There was absolutely no point in disturbing you for a matter of two nights which I can spend perfectly comfortably at a friend's place. Diana is panicking unnecessarily. When I need to come back, I will tell you.'

'Are you sure?' she said doubtfully. 'It would make us feel dreadfully uncomfortable to find that you'd put yourself out for us to that extent.'

'I never put myself out for anyone. My convenience is always my first consideration, I assure you.'

'Now that I do *not* believe.'

'Because it's your nature to think well of people. Mine is the reverse. I suspect other people's motives and my own are always based on self-interest. I shouldn't be where I am if it were not so.'

'I can't see how it's of the least advantage to you to have lent us your delightful flat,' she pointed out.

He considered this for a moment. 'My father started

life as a butcher's errand boy. Perhaps it pleases me to be on friendly terms with a baroness,' he suggested.

Patience smiled at him. 'That might have been the case a hundred or even fifty years ago, but not now. Titles have long lost their glamour. To be a peer or peeress is not nearly as fashionable as to be seen on television regularly—and I'm sure you could arrange that, if you wished to. I'm sure your kindness to us has nothing to do with social climbing.'

'No, in fact it hasn't,' he admitted. 'But nor is it entirely disinterested.' He looked at Diana. 'I wonder if, instead of making tea, you would mind going for a stroll for half an hour? There's something I should like to discuss with your mother in private.'

It was such an odd, unexpected request that she was taken aback.

'I shan't tire or upset her, I promise you,' Reid added quietly.

'Of course not. I'm not such a poor thing as you two seem to think,' said Lady Marriott. 'A little more fresh air will do you good, darling. And when you come back we'll have tea and some of Mrs Lane's gingerbread.'

'All right.' Trying not to show her disquiet at this very strange turn of events, Diana glanced at her watch. 'I'll be back at half past three.'

All the time she was walking round the park, she was racking her brains for a reason why Reid should want to speak to her mother privately. It could only have to do with the Abbey but, since he had given his word that he didn't want to buy it, what else could he have in mind?

Although her mother had pooh-poohed his claim to being a self-centred man, Diana thought that, in most things, he probably was.

Sandro Oneto had suspected him of intending to add her to the list of his past affairs. But whatever he was discussing with Patience could have nothing to do with that. It must be a matter of business. But what sort of business?

She returned to the flat on the dot of half past three, but found her mother alone.

'Reid has gone. He's coming back later,' said Patience. 'Have you put the kettle on, darling?'

'Not yet. I will in a minute. What did he want to talk about that he couldn't discuss in front of me?'

'Make the tea first, and then we can talk while we have it.'

Diana went to the kitchen. Her mother's placid manner suggested that whatever had come up in her absence could not have been anything too momentous. Now that it was about to be satisfied, her curiosity subsided a little.

When she returned to the sitting-room with the tea tray, Patience put aside her needlework.

'Reid will be back here at seven. I shall have supper in bed, leaving you two alone. This evening it's you he wants to see privately.'

'What for? What is all this, Mummy?'

'Can't you guess, darling? You're usually so quick on the uptake. Surely you must have an inkling?' Her mother's smile held affectionate teasing.

'I have no idea. Do stop being mysterious and tell me.'

'He wanted to see me alone to ask my permission to propose to you. He wants to marry you, Diana.'

'You can't be serious!'

Diana's voice was a hoarse croak of incredulity. If she hadn't already put the tray down, she would have dropped it.

Flopping backwards into a chair, she exclaimed, 'The man must be crazy. Marry him? I hardly know him!'

'He wouldn't have been so precipitate if it hadn't been for my illness and our other difficulties. He wants to take care of you, and it's very difficult to do that unless you're married. You like him, don't you? I like him immensely.'

But you, darling Mummy, have already messed up your life by liking my father, was Diana's thought.

She kept it to herself, saying only, 'I don't know that I do. I haven't made up my mind about him. I know he's been very kind, but he himself said it wasn't entirely disinterested. I think what he wants is not me

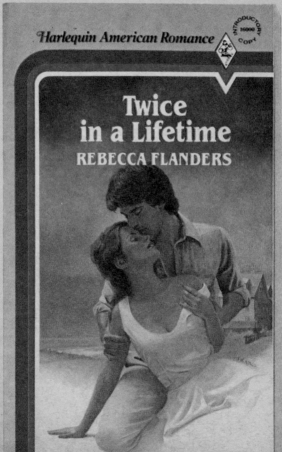

Proudly introducing
Harlequin
American Romance™
with this FREE book offer.

Experience *Harlequin American Romance*...

with this special introductory FREE book offer.

◀ SEE EXCITING DETAILS INSIDE

Send no money. Mail this card and receive this new, full-length *Harlequin American Romance* novel absolutely FREE.

but the Abbey, and this is a cheap way to get it.'

'Oh, no!' Lady Marriott looked shocked. 'I'm sure that has nothing to do with it. He's fallen in love with you, darling. One could see that he was very much attracted the first time we met him. He hardly took his eyes off you.'

'Did he tell you he was in love with me?'

'He'll tell *you* that tonight, I imagine. I suggested he took you out to dinner, but he thought you wouldn't be happy at leaving me on my own, and a public restaurant isn't the ideal place to propose.'

'I don't want to be proposed to,' Diana said swiftly. 'I don't want to marry anyone.'

Her mother poured out the tea before she said gently, 'It's come as rather a shock. You need time to think it over. Naturally I shouldn't dream of urging you to marry anyone you didn't like and respect and find attractive. But I have to admit that it would be a great relief to me to know that—if the operation isn't successful—you wouldn't be left on your own with such a heavy reponsibility.'

Diana sprang out of the chair and rushed to put her arms round her.

'The operation *will* be successful. You're going to get well, I know it. A few months from now and you'll be as fit as you ever were.'

Patience returned her embrace. 'I hope so, dearest. I hope so. But even if I do pull through—and I'll do my best, I promise you that—we shall still have enormous problems. Reid would take care of all those, and he'd give you a wonderful life. You'd have all that money can buy, and it's not to be sniffed at, Diana. High-minded people may say that money never buys happiness. But, unless you're a nun or a saint, you can't be happy without it. You know that as well as I do. We were always a great deal happier when your father was in funds than when he was in debt. And we weren't very happy in Spain with the cost of living going up, and our small income standing still.'

Diana withdrew her arms but stayed beside her on

the sofa. Whenever Patience referred to the possibility that she might die, it terrified her to think of going on alone without her mother.

They had always been exceptionally close and, in recent years, more like sisters than parent and child. They had no other close relations. Her father's parents were dead and he had been their only child. On her mother's side there were some distant cousins who belonged to a cadet branch of the family, but Patience had never met them.

Without her mother, Diana was entirely alone in the world—a daunting prospect even if she and Lady Marriott had not got on well with each other. With the tie between them being a strong one, it was something not to be contemplated.

'Anyway, Reid won't expect you to give him an answer tonight,' Patience went on. 'He realises it's all very sudden, and that someone of your age can't make such a serious decision as quickly as someone of his. But I wouldn't turn him down flat, my dear. Let him put his case for himself, and then think about it. He won't rush you. Now drink your tea before it gets cold.'

Diana did as she was told and, pressed by her mother, even ate a slice of the housekeeper's gingerbread. But she didn't taste it; she was too bemused.

'Why did he speak to you first?' she asked presently.

'Partly to test my reaction, and partly to find out if I had any insight into your feelings. I told him I had no idea how you would react, but that I would welcome him as a son-in-law. It's not only his financial standing which commends him to me. I like him as a man. I see in him all the qualities which were so lacking in your father. Reid is reliable, which poor Denzil never was.'

'How do you know he's reliable? We know very little about him, Mummy. He says he is rich, but how do we know? Because he has this flat, and an Aston Martin? It could all be done by mirrors. Daddy could give the impression of being rolling in money.'

'Yes, that's true, I have to admit. He could. But

staying in an expensive hotel for a few days, in order to create an impression of affluence, is a different matter from owning a flat like this one, or even leasing it. Mrs Lane has been working here for several years, and from things she has told me about him, I'm sure he's completely above board. He even spoke of a marriage settlement which he'd make to secure your future, should anything happen to him.'

'Very businesslike. Not very romantic,' was Diana's comment.

'I imagine he's reserving that for later,' said her mother, with a smile.

The thought of Reid trying to kiss her threw Diana into a panic. And he wouldn't just try. He'd succeed. Before she knew what was happening, she would find that wide, sensual mouth pressed to her unwilling lips, and if she didn't respond he would probably kiss her until she did.

'I'm going to go and have my bath,' said Lady Marriott. 'If we're eating at seven-thirty, the kidneys should go in the oven about five minutes to seven. I only hope he likes kidneys. At least they'll stretch, which the meal we had last night wouldn't.'

As her mother left the room, Diana looked at her watch. It was now four o'clock. In three hours Reid would be back and, although her mother would be in another room, they would be more alone together than they ever had been before. If he wanted to take her in his arms, there would be nothing to stop him.

Later her mother tried to persuade her to dress in something more glamorous than the jersey and trousers which she usually wore in the evening. But Diana jibbed at arraying herself for the occasion, even in the pale green silk dress in which Reid had first seen her.

She found it acutely embarrassing to know in advance what he meant to ask her. To doll herself up would be to imply her willingness to receive his proposal—which was very far from being the case.

By the time he was due to arrive, she was inwardly quaking with nervousness. For the first time in her life she even felt angry with her mother for allowing this preposterous situation to come about. It was nothing short of archaic for a man to seek parental permission before making a formal proposal. It just didn't happen any more. The normal thing was for two people to fall in love and settle the matter between themselves. Reid was reviving formalities which were as long out of date as the concept of a marriage of convenience.

Yet she had to admit that hers was precisely the situation which had led to so many marriages of convenience in the past; except that the impoverished owner of the historic house had usually been the bridegroom, and the possessor of wealth the bride.

Patience was already in bed when the doorbell heralded Reid's arrival. Taking a firm grip on herself, she went to admit him.

Appearing as relaxed as she was tense, he said, 'Hello, Diana,' and strolled into the lobby with his hands behind his back.

She bade him a stilted good evening, and closed the door behind him. As she turned, he produced a tight, leaf-framed bunch of violets.

She had never been given violets before, indeed any flowers.

'Th-thank you.' She lifted them to her nose to smell their sweetness. 'M . . . lovely. I'll put them in water. I believe you know where the drinks are.'

With this feeble attempt at a joke, she turned to go into the kitchen.

He caught her lightly by the shoulder, making her pivot. His other hand tilted her chin. He stooped to kiss her on the mouth.

It was a very gentle kiss, the merest brushing of lips. Nothing like Diego's first kiss, but more like the kisses exchanged by people of her grandparents' generation.

Reid straightened. He was smiling slightly. And then, before Diana had recovered from the surprise of it, he drew her to him with both arms and kissed her again, much more thoroughly.

At last he let her go. 'That proves one thing,' he said,

in a satisfied tone. 'We're going to enjoy kissing each other—which is quite important, don't you think?'

He held open the kitchen door, and Diana stumbled through it, both wits and senses in disarray.

He spoke as if the matter were a fait accompli, she thought, a few minutes later, when her pulse was beginning to decelerate.

But it had been shock, not pleasure, which had made her submit to his embrace, she told herself. *She* had not enjoyed it particularly, even if he had. Perhaps it had been less unpleasant than being kissed by some men might have been; but that wasn't to say that she wanted to repeat the experience.

And yet as she found a small jar and filled it with water for the violets, her hands were still trembling and she could feel her heart beating.

Reid had just selected a record from his large collection when she joined him in the sitting-room.

She had looked through his records and found that his taste ranged from Haydn to Diana Ross. She hadn't played any of them. His music centre looked dauntingly complicated.

His choice was a piano recording which she didn't recognise. He turned the volume control to a level where the music was audible but not intrusive.

'Now ... what can I get you to drink?' he asked, turning towards her.

'Oh ... I meant to get myself some orange juice. It's in the fridge. What are you having? Shall I bring you some ice?'

'No, thanks. I'm having sherry—*not* on the rocks,' he added dryly, his tone making it clear what he thought of that innovation.

Diana escaped to the kitchen and poured herself some unsweetened orange juice.

When she rejoined him, he said, 'You're obviously very nervous. Why?'

'*Why?*' she expostulated. 'Who wouldn't be, in the circumstances? I'm not used to ... to people asking my mother if they can marry me. Frankly, I think you must be mad. This is only the fourth time we've met.'

'Some people recognise their soulmatés the first time they see them,' he replied, with a gleam of amusement.

'I don't believe in soulmates, and I shouldn't think you do either. Whatever your motive for this is, I'm quite sure it isn't romentic,' she told him bluntly.

'No, you're right, it isn't,' he agreed. 'Shall we sit down?'—with a gesture at two comfortable armchairs placed on either side of a lamp table.

'I think marriage is far too important to be based on the state of mind known as being in love,' he continued, when they were seated. 'The fact that it is, is the reason for the high divorce rate. In my opinion, for a man and woman to live together for perhaps fifty years calls for a much more solid foundation than romantic love. I want to stay married. Don't you?'

'Yes, I suppose so—if I wanted to marry. At present I don't,' she answered flatly.

'Understandable. You're still very young. If you were a free agent, you could afford to wait a few years. But you're not. You have the future of the Abbey to consider. In my case, I've waited long enough. As it is I shall be in my fifties by the time the eldest of my children are grown up.'

'How many children are you planning to have?'

'As many, within reason, as you are prepared to give me. Certainly not less than three.'

'Has it occurred to you that I might not be able to have any?' she asked, with an edge in her voice.

'An unlikely contingency. I might be infertile myself. But there aren't many couples who, aided by modern science, can't reproduce if they try hard enough. In most cases it would be sensible if they didn't try,' Reid added sardonically. 'The world is already overcrowded.'

'But you feel entitled to add a quiverful of little Lockwoods to the crush?'

'Certainly. At present most intelligent people are limiting themselves to one or at the most two children, while the unintelligent breed with abandon,' he answered. 'That creates a serious imbalance—too many followers and not enough leaders. I'm not proposing to burden the State with my offspring. They will be my responsibility. And, I hope, our other important contribution to the future of the country.'

'Our other contribution?' she echoed perplexedly.

'The first being to put your mother's estate on its feet so that yet another historic house isn't lost to posterity. Too many have been demolished already; or, if not demolished, diverted from their traditional use as family houses.'

He set aside his glass of sherry and leaned forward in the chair, his arms resting on his long thighs and his strong fingers interlaced. Suddenly his rather inscrutable eyes were alight with a burning enthusiasm.

'I told you I had a project which I wasn't ready to discuss. It was that, between us, we should put new life into the Abbey in every sense of the word. I should like to see it become a self-supporting community as all the great estates used to be. One day I'll take you to Williamsburg in America where the whole colonial part of the city has been revived and, with it, many eighteenth century crafts. It was financed by one of the Rockefellers, and the object of the exercise is "that the future may learn from the past". On a smaller scale, we could do the same thing at the Abbey. The village has no bakery now, but an old boy I talked to in the pub told me the Abbey had bread ovens which would still be usable. We could make the estate an enclave of crops grown without chemicals, and livestock reared in natural conditions. We could even try to re-introduce the wild flowers and wild creatures which modern farming destroys. We have the land and the means to make ourselves a private world. In effect, the best of both worlds—past and present.'

Diana could not help but be stirred by the fervour in his voice and indeed by the idea he outlined.

Reid had leaned back in his chair and was sipping his sherry, watching her.

After a little, she said, 'I agree it's an exciting concept, but it's not a basis for marriage.'

'I believe it is. A shared, continuing interest is exactly what most marriages lack. Children provide it to some extent, but they aren't, or shouldn't be, the hub of their parents' existence. They grow up and set out on their own lives, and it's then, very often, that a weak marriage falls apart. But a couple who run a business together, or who are members of the same profession, or even who are both keen gardeners or golfers or whatever, they have a much better chance of staying married.'

Diana could not dispute that there was some force in what he said.

'I—I must go and attend to our meal,' she said, jumping up.

'Can I help you?'

'No thank you. There's very little to do.' She hurried away.

Her mind was in such a whirl that it was difficult to concentrate on the final preparations for their supper. With the kidneys in their rich gravy, they were having baked potatoes and cabbage. This she had already shredded and it needed only a few minutes' cooking before being thoroughly drained, then shaken with a big knob of butter and dredged with black pepper and nutmeg.

The table and her mother's tray were already laid. It wasn't long before she called Reid to the table.

'It's a very simple supper.' she warned him. 'Would you start serving the kidneys while I bring in the vegetables. A rather small helping for my mother, please.'

'Is everything all right?' asked Lady Marriott, when her daughter took in her tray.

'Yes . . . fine.' Diana forced a smile. What else could she say?

In her absence Reid had helped her as well as himself to the vegetables. He was waiting behind her chair.

Having pushed it in for her, he said, 'Don't you drink wine with your meals here? I'm sure you did in Spain.'

'Not always. I'm sorry: what with one thing and

another it didn't occur to me that you might like some.'

'It won't take a moment to open a bottle.'

He disappeared, but in less than half a minute was back with a bottle of red wine, three glasses and a corkscrew. The plates being hot, the slight delay while he deftly removed the cork, and she took a glass to her mother, did no harm to the food on them.

Reid seemed hungry. Diana had seldom felt less like eating.

'This isn't one of Mrs Lane's dishes. It must be yours,' he remarked, after sampling the kidneys in silence for a minute or two.

'It's one of my mother's specialities which she taught me to make.'

He picked up his wineglass and held it towards her. 'To us.'

Diana took hold of her glass, but not to respond to his gesture. Nervously twisting the stem, she said, 'You're taking too much for granted. You've been very kind, and I'm grateful, but not to the extent of being bulldozed into marriage.'

'For the time being I'm only pressing you to agree to an engagement,' he answered. 'I shouldn't expect you to marry me until after your mother leaves hospital. That, I gather, won't be until about twelve weeks after the operation, which will give you plenty of time to adjust to the idea. Meanwhile I shall have the right to lighten your burdens as much as possible.'

'But if you do that—if you put in hand the plans you spoke of earlier—then I shall be committed,' she pointed out. 'An engagement *is* a commitment. Not as binding as marriage, perhaps, but not something to be taken on lightly.'

Reid drank some wine. 'You told me the day we had lunch at The Nun's Head that you wanted to concentrate all your time and energy on the Abbey, and not to think about marriage until you were in your late twenties. But if you want children to succeed you, you'd do better to have them while you're young. Naturally, as my wife you would have a nanny as well as other staff to relieve you of all the routine chores. You could concentrate on whatever interested you most. I can give you anything you want, Diana.'

'Except love.'

'That, too, probably—in time. We shouldn't be the first couple to marry for practical reasons and later develop a strong affection for each other. Do you remember telling me about your mother's views on privilege and responsibility?'

She nodded.

'Whether you wish it or not,' he went on, 'you're the heir to an ancient title and an historic house. That imposes a duty to safeguard them. You couldn't allow your heart to rule your head even if you were a romantic by nature, which you assure me you aren't.'

'I also remember something you said earlier today— that your motives are always based on self-interest,' she pointed out. 'Would *your* sense of responsibility restrain you if, later, you were attracted to other women? I may not be a romantic, but any wife feels humiliated when her husband is unfaithful to her.'

She was thinking of her mother, but she would not confide that to him. She was also thinking of the women Sandro Oneto had mentioned, only one of them by name.

'That would depend on you,' said Reid. 'Generally speaking, husbands are only unfaithful when their wives are unloving.'

'Or that is their husbands' excuse,' she said dryly.

She could not believe that her mother, having given up so much to run away with him, had ever been unloving to her father.

Unless . . . unless she had married him with her head full of poetry and dreams, only to be cruelly disillusioned by a lover who had not matched up to her girlish expectations.

What if I'd been married to Diego before I found out what he was really like? she thought, with a twinge of the old pain. Could I have gone on being warm and loving towards him? She knew the answer was no. But then she had never truly loved him, nor he her.

'In a few cases, yes,' said Reid in response to her comment. 'But not in the majority. Most of us subscribe to the couplet—Do not adultery commit, advantage rarely comes of it.'

By this time they had both finished eating. As she rose and took away their plates, he followed her with the vegetable dishes.

'I think you're taking rather a negative attitude,' he said, in the kitchen. 'In any life-changing scheme, it's wise to offset the snags against the advantages. But most people consider the credits before the debits.'

Diana opened the fridge and took out a bowl of fruit salad.

'If this were a business proposition, I should probably take a more positive attitude. I like your scheme as far as it relates to the Abbey. It's the personal aspect which bothers me. I'm going to get Mummy's tray,' she added, before he could answer.

Lady Marriott was watching the television installed in a section of the wardrobe and controlled from the bed.

'That was delicious, darling. Did Reid enjoy it?'

'He seemed to. There's some cabbage and potato left over. We can have bubble-and-squeak for lunch tomorrow.'

How calm I sound, thought Diana. She was calmer now. The first shock had begun to wear off and her hands were steady again.

Returning to the kitchen, she found that Reid had filled one of the three fruit bowls she had put out on the worktop.

'I can't find any cream,' he said.

'We have yogurt instead. Do you normally eat cream and butter? Most men seem to avoid them nowadays.'

'As I'm not overweight or under-exercised, I eat everything—in moderation.'

It was not until they were seated at the table again that, resuming their earlier conversation, she said, 'Why

can't it be done as a business partnership?—This plan
you have for the estate? you could live in part of the
Abbey, and we could live in the other.'

Reid shook his head. 'That's not what I want. To live
there as a bachelor wouldn't suit me as well as living
here; and to introduce another woman—even if I knew
anyone suitable—would be to complicate matters,
perhaps disastrously. No, I want a full stake in the
project, and I want my children to grow up feeling they
belong there.'

Diana could see he was not to be budged.

'To me it's a crazy idea . . . but I'll think it over,' she
said slowly.

'By all means. I didn't expect you to make up your
mind straight away. I didn't myself. I thought it out
very carefully. Now that we've dealt with the serious
business on tonight's agenda, how about a little more
wine?' he suggested with a smile.

They had their coffee in the sitting-room where,
learning that she had never made use of it, Reid
explained the controls of his music centre.

Presently, leaving him to see if her mother would like
some more of the mint tea which was now her
substitute for coffee, she found Lady Marriott asleep.

'But I'm afraid she'll wake up later on. She spends
half the night reading your Macaulay's *History of
England*,' she told him, when she returned to the
sitting-room.

'I imagine you won't sleep very soundly tonight,' he
remarked, with a quizzical gleam. 'But it's a mistake to
dwell on decisions in bed. Mine are usually made in the
morning, after a shower and breakfast, when the mind
is at its clearest. The brain doesn't function well during
the night watches.'

'And obviously you never allow your heart to
influence you,' she returned, with a touch of astrin-
gency.

'In small things—certainly. Not where major issues
are concerned. Reason is a better guide than feeling.
Which is not to say that I lack feelings; merely that I've

learnt to keep them under control.'

He turned to the bookshelves. 'Which of my books have you been reading? Or has none of them appealed to you?'

'I've read most of the travel books. I enjoyed *Slow Boats to China*. I thought *The Last Wilderness* disappointing.'

'So did I,' he agreed.

On this safe subject they passed the next half hour.

Had it not been for her fear that, at any moment, he might pounce on her and repeat the disturbing kiss he had forced on her when he arrived, she would have enjoyed their conversation.

But when Reid took his leave, rather early, he did not kiss her.

'I expect to be away for at least another week and possibly longer. When I do return I shall expect you to have made up your mind,' he told her, before saying goodnight.

After he had gone, Diana put the supper things in the dishwasher and would have gone to bed had she not seen a chink of light round her mother's door.

'Is there anything I can get for you, Mummy?' she asked, having tapped on the door and found Patience reading again.

'No, thank you, darling. Has Reid gone?'

'Yes.' Diana sat down on the foot of the bed. 'You were wrong about him being in love with me. What he wants is more like a merger—with the possibility that we might grow fond of each other as time went on.'

'And you turned him down?' Patience asked.

'No . . . no, I didn't. He's given me till he gets back to make up my mind.'

Her mother was silent for some moments. Then she said, 'No one was more romantic than I when I was a girl. Goodness knows why. My parents' marriage certainly wasn't an example of connubial bliss. My mother had been in love with my father at the beginning, but he was always a difficult man and, in the end, a very cruel one.'

'You mean he actually ill-treated her?'

'Not physically, no. But he desperately wanted a male heir, and when she had nothing but girls—she'd had two miscarriages before I was born—he blamed her. Apparently he had had a son by someone else, and it made him very bitter to be "saddled", as he put it, with a wife who could only produce daughters. For the last few years before she died, they led a cat-and-dog life.'

'How beastly for you!'

'It wasn't very pleasant but, as all my loyalty was to her, at least I wasn't torn in two directions as some children are. Having had parents at odds with each other is one of the reasons why I tried, as far as possible, to keep Denzil's and my differences from blighting your growing up years.'

'Were you very unhappy?' asked Diana. 'I know he was a rotten husband, but you seemed to be fond of him in spite of it.'

'I'd burnt my boats by running away with him. I had to see it through,' said Patience. 'But oh, how often I wished I'd listened to my mother when she told me that falling in love with a man was almost always a snare and a delusion. *She* had been brought up by her grandmother who was of the Edwardian generation, and they believed in marrying for a life-style, not for anything as evanescent as love. Imagine how much worse my mother's life would have been if she hadn't had a separate bedroom, and her own sitting-room, and no money worries.'

'I suppose so,' Diana said thoughtfully. 'Do you think affection *can* grow where it doesn't exist from the beginning?'

'I'm sure it can. In fact I believe that, providing he isn't actually repulsive to her, a woman can learn to love any man who is kind and considerate. This business of "falling in love" is really only a matter of being intensely attracted. That's why—although I used not to approve of it—I think now that living together is really rather a good idea.'

'Do you?' her daughter asked, in surprise.

'Yes, because a purely sexual attraction is something which dies down quite quickly if a couple have nothing else in common. If Denzil and I had been able to live together for a few months, I should have realised we were wrong for each other. In less time . . . in just a few weeks.'

'You mean you fell out of love as quickly as that?' Diana exclaimed, in dismay.

She had no idea that her mother's disillusionment had set in so early.

'I had such foolish ideas,' Patience replied, with a sigh. 'I expected the heights of ecstasy, and when . . . when it wasn't like that, I felt badly let down. Probably a lot of brides did. Perhaps they still do. But in most cases there are compensations to make up for that particular disappointment. In my case there weren't.'

Although, in earlier years, she had always answered her daughter's questions in a straightforward, open manner, it was plain that she felt uncomfortable discussing such things in a personal context. By tacit consent they changed the direction of the conversation and, not more than five minutes later, Diana kissed her goodnight.

It was, as Reid had forecast, a long time before she slept. At one o'clock in the morning she was still recapitulating all the reasons which he and her mother had advanced in favour of their marriage.

All she had to set against them was her own irrational conviction that a marriage devoid of love was as unlikely to survive as one based on romantic illusions.

Her dilemma stopped being important the following afternoon when, much sooner than they had expected, Lady Marriott was hurried to the hospital because, as the result of a road accident, a heart and lungs which matched hers were available for the transplant.

Diana was allowed to stay with her until she was taken to the operating theatre.

'See you tomorrow, darling,' Patience said confidently, before they wheeled her away.

But, as the rubber-wheeled trolley rolled away down the corridor, Diana knew it was possible that they had said goodbye for ever; that tomorrow she would be alone in the world.

Considering its nature, the operation was not a long one. It would take only four hours to make three vital disconnections, divert her mother's blood flow to a heart-lung machine, remove the diseased organs and replace them with the healthy ones donated by a young motor-cyclist whose grief-stricken parents had agreed to the transplant.

As the flat was not far from the hospital, Diana had been advised to wait there. But she could not bear to leave the building where her mother's life was at stake.

With seemingly interminable slowness, the hands of the waiting-room clock crept round the dial. Ten minutes ... twenty ... thirty.

The first three hours were the longest hours of her life. There was no one else waiting with her, and she found it impossible to read. She could only sit, restless and tense, or wander nervously about, imagining what was happening in the brightly lit operating theatre.

About ten minutes after a nurse had brought her a cup of strong tea, she heard the squeak of the door and looked up to see Reid striding in.

'What are you doing here?' she asked, astonished.

'Mrs Lane telephoned me in Paris. I came as soon as I could. You look very tired, my poor girl.'

'You mean ... you came back to be with me?'

'You need someone to be with you. Is there anyone else better qualified?'

'No ... no one,' she said, her voice breaking. 'Oh, Reid ... thank you! Thank you for coming. I felt ... so alone ... I can't tell you.'

'I can imagine. But you're not alone any more and, as Sister tells me there's no possibility of your mother coming down from the theatre for at least another hour, I'm taking you out for something to eat. They'll know where we are if you're wanted.'

In a small restaurant, close to the hospital, he ordered without consulting her. Although she had thought she wasn't hungry, when the food came she found that she was.

Reid was still with her, several hours later, when the Sister in charge of the floor came to tell her that her mother was expected to recover consciousness, if only for a few moments, and would be reassured by seeing her daughter.

Although she had been prepared for it, it was still a shock to see Patience lying with closed eyes, deathly pale and surrounded by medical apparatus.

When her mother did come to, there was no way of telling if she recognised Diana's smiling eyes above the mask which, for some time to come, all her attendants and visitors would have to wear.

Told by Lady Marriott's surgeon that the operation had gone well, and that she should now go home and rest, Diana allowed Reid to take her back to the flat.

There, emotionally drained by the long vigil, and assured that he would not let her sleep too long, she undressed and fell into bed.

Afterwards, Diana did not know how she would have survived the following weeks without Reid's support.

Although the operation was over, there was still the ever-present danger that Lady Marriott's body might reject the transplanted organs, or that—in spite of the precautions against it—an ordinary infection might invade her weakened system and kill her.

For three weeks after the operation, Diana never left the hospital without wondering if she might be urgently recalled some time during the hours before her next visit.

During this time Reid never referred to the ultimatum he had given her before going to Paris. She was still in possession of the flat, and he was staying round the corner at the Ritz Hotel. It seemed a crazy arrangement, but he wouldn't hear of her moving out, and she let herself be overruled.

Every morning he walked with her in the park, and every evening he had dinner with her. Sometimes he came with her to see her mother and, although Lady Marriott made no direct reference to this, Diana could see that it pleased her when they came together. Obviously, in her mother's mind, their marriage was a fait accompli.

There came a day, about a month after the operation, when Patience seemed so much improved that Diana could at least believe the worst was over.

As they were leaving the hospital, Reid told her he had tickets for a new play. When they separated in St James's, she found herself looking forward to an evening out.

As it was opening night, and she guessed they would either be in the front of the stalls or the dress circle, she decided to put on the black chiffon dress which her mother had bought years ago in Paris, during one of her father's affluent phases. The dress had a built-in slip of black silk crêpe-de-chine which left her shoulders and arms bare under the filmy chiffon. The hem of the skirt was narrowly bound with black satin, as was the round neckline which fastened with rouleaux ties to match the ties at the wrists.

She decided to wear her hair brushed back from her face and pinned in a coil. Somehow junk jewellery seemed wrong with the beautifully made *couture* dress, so she put on the small, fine gold hoops she had had since her earlobes were pierced for her seventeenth birthday.

Her shoes were Italian-made high-heeled black velvet pumps with cutaway sides, also bought long ago by Lady Marriott. Luckily they took the same size. Accustomed as she was to going bare-legged or wearing trousers, Diana felt very strange wearing cobwebby pantihose over her micro-briefs.

She had wondered if Reid might have changed into a dinner jacket, but evidently this was not de rigueur, as he came to collect her in a dark suit with a rather dashing striped shirt and a plain tie.

'I haven't seen you looking so sophisticated since the day you arrived in something green,' he remarked, as she led him into the sitting-room. 'You know it's almost a crime to camouflage those lovely long legs with jeans and track shoes. You should always wear skirts and high heels.'

This was a reversion to the way he had looked at her and talked to her at the beginning. She guessed that, before the evening was over, he was going to insist on an answer to his proposal; but it was a decision she had shelved while her mother's life was at risk.

The play was a fast-paced comedy which, most of the time, stopped her worrying about what to say to him later. Nevertheless it didn't make her completely oblivious to the broad shoulder inches from hers or the long hard thigh parallel with her softer leg.

She noticed, too, that he had a much nicer laugh than the bray-like guffaws of some of the men in the audience.

There was so much to like about him, and he had been extraordinarily kind at a time when she had badly needed moral support. But somehow her gratitude for that did not quite cancel out her first impression of him as a hard, tough man, or her memory of Sandro Oneto telling Reid that he could hurt 'this little girl' if he treated her like his other women.

After the play he took her to dine in a small, quiet restaurant where the tables were secluded by partitions. Red-shaded wall lights and table lamps added to the intimate atmosphere.

For much of the meal they discussed the play and the actors' performances. Eventually the subject was exhausted and, after a pause in which she tried vainly to think of another topic which would stave off more personal matters, Reid said, 'Are you going to marry me, Diana?'

Her long silky lashes fluttered nervously before she raised her gaze to meet his.

'I—I think there are things you should know before you ask me that again,' she said, in a low tone.

He lifted an eyebrow. 'For example?'

She gave a swift glance around them. None of the staff was within earshot and the four people in the opposite booth were engrossed in their own conversation.

Her eyes returned to his face. 'I . . . I'm not a virgin,' she told him.

For an instant she thought she saw a flash of surprise and anger in his eyes, but perhaps it was only her fancy. Almost immediately he said, 'Neither am I.'

'I didn't expect that you would be, but you might have thought that I was.'

'Yes, I did, as it happens. However——' he paused and gave a slight shrug, 'it's not a matter of great moment, provided that your past is past. Women have an unfortunate tendency to hanker after their old loves.'

'That certainly isn't true in my case. I wish I'd never set eyes on him,' Diana admitted bitterly.

'Was it your first affair?'

She nodded. 'My only affair. I—I haven't been promiscuous.'

A hint of amusement touched his mouth. 'You don't have to tell me that,' he said dryly. 'I've kissed you—remember?'

She flushed. 'That's the other thing you ought to know. I—I'm not a very demonstrative person.'

The dark eyebrow tilted upwards again. 'You appear to have an extremely affectionate relationship with your mother, and I wouldn't have described your first encounter with Bertie as undemonstrative.'

'That's different. I meant . . . with men.'

'Perhaps that was his fault,' he said.

She fingered the stem of her glass. 'Or perhaps I'm not very hot-blooded. It could be a hereditary trait. I didn't suspect it until recently, but I think now there may have been a reason for my father's infidelities.' She lifted her chin and looked him squarely in the eyes. 'It's better to be straight with you now. I shouldn't like you to feel I'd accepted your proposal under false pretences.'

'Am I to take it from that, if these revelations make no difference to my attitude, you do accept my proposal?'

Diana held her breath.

Years ago, when she was about nine, she had climbed to the top-most diving board at a large swimming pool. As she looked down, her courage had failed her. It looked a frighteningly long way. Supposing she did a belly flop? She had wanted to withdraw to a lower board, but pride had forced her to launch herself into the air.

This time it wasn't the fear of being thought a coward by the spectators that warred with her terror of committing her future to the man on the other side of the table. There would be private embarrassment but no public humiliation if she backed down at the last moment. Now it was the need to protect her mother from worry and insecurity which drove her to take a metaphorical plunge every bit as terrifying as that first scary dive from the high board.

'Yes,' she said huskily. 'Yes.'

'Good: in that case the matter is settled.'

CHAPTER FIVE

HE beckoned a waiter and she caught the name Dom Ruinart, which turned out to be champagne.

'To our joint future,' said Reid, as he lifted his glass.

'To our joint future,' she echoed.

It sounded like a business deal; which, of course, was precisely what it was. There would be no point in pretending otherwise.

On top of the wine she had already drunk, the second glass of champagne made her feel a little lightheaded.

'Shall we walk back? It's not very far,' she suggested, when he had paid the bill.

'Can you walk in those shoes you're wearing?'

'If you don't mind not going as fast as usual.'

'Not at all.'

The night air, which Diana had hoped would dispel the lightheadedness, seemed to have the reverse effect. She was glad when Reid took her hand. He must guess that she was feeling slightly hazy.

Some of the shop windows they passed were still alight. Many, presumably in support of the energy-saving campaign, were not. The street lamps turned the unlighted panes into shadowy mirrors in which their reflections strolled through the night like two romantic-looking strangers. A tall, chic, ashen-fair girl—which was not how she saw herself—and a man with a strong, rawboned profile which seemed out of place in a city, and out of time in this century.

A merchant adventurer in the days when men made their fortunes in more direct and exciting ways than by shrewd investments—that was who the reflected man looked like, even though he was wearing modern clothes.

'I'll see you to your door,' he said when, observed by the ever-watchful porter, they crossed the lobby to the lifts.

Did he mean to kiss her goodnight? Diana wondered, her insides beginning to churn.

As the lift rose, she felt him watching her. 'Not my door—your door,' she corrected him.

'Our door, as soon as your mother is fit again. Tomorrow morning we'll go shopping for an engagement ring. Have you any idea what you'd like?'

'I've never thought about it.'

'Think about it tonight. I'll pick you up at ten.'

Although she stepped from the lift before he did, Reid moved ahead of her in the corridor and had his own key in the lock when she reached the door. He pushed it open and felt for the light switch.

'May I come in for five minutes?'

'Of course,' she said, her mouth dry.

He stood aside for her to enter. She walked through to the sitting-room and touched the switch which illuminated one of the several table lamps.

'I must admit I shan't be sorry to stand on my own heels. I'm not used to these high—*oh!*'

Her exclamation was in reaction to finding herself encircled by Reid's left arm, while his right hand searched for the pins securing her hair.

'This is very elegant, but I prefer your hair loose.'

As it tumbled free, his hand cupped the back of her head and he stooped to kiss her; not on the mouth, but all over the rest of her face, his warm lips exploring the chamois-soft warmth of her cheeks, the sweep of her eyebrows, the sensitive skin of her eyelids. And all the time he was kissing her, his other arm clasped her against him with her hands trapped between her breasts and the rock-like wall of his chest.

At first she was passive; submitting because she had no choice. She had given him the right to do this to her. But slowly, little by little, the caressing mouth changed her compliance to a tingle of unwilling response.

Not ungently, Reid took hold of her hair and made her bend back her head, exposing the curve of her throat from her chain to the neck of her dress. His lips travelled down to the hollow just above her collarbones, then retraced their route back to the pulse point under her jaw.

He seemed to know all the places which sent little tremors through her; tremors which increased in intensity as his mouth returned to her face and she waited to feel its pressure on her quivering lips.

When, suddenly, he let her go, it was not only a surprise but a disappointment. The interruption was only momentary. Catching her hands, he placed them high up on his shoulders and, a second later, caught her to him in an altogether stronger embrace which sealed her against his powerful body while his mouth came down firmly on hers in a long, possessive kiss.

When it ended, her arms were round his neck and she was clinging to him. Stunned by the strength of the feelings he had aroused in her, she tried to draw quickly away. He wouldn't let her go—or not beyond his arms' reach. His hands at the back of her waist, he looked down into her startled, bemused face.

'Not demonstrative, Diana?' he asked, with a gleam of teasing. 'You could have fooled me. Goodnight. Sleep well.'

Before she could catch her breath to stammer a reply, he had left her, closing the outer door quietly behind him.

By the time she was ready to climb into bed, her disturbed emotions had calmed down, and her head was as clear as it had been at the outset of the evening.

Clearly, Reid had left the flat confident that, whatever had happened in the past, *he* was not going to have any difficulty in making her respond to him. What he didn't realise was that, two years ago, she had responded to Diego—had been swept away by his kisses to the point of letting him seduce her.

She remembered what Patience had said to her on the night of Reid's down-to-earth proposal.

I had such foolish ideas. I expected the heights of ecstasy and when it wasn't like that I felt badly let down. Probably a lot of brides did. Perhaps they still do.

Diana had not been a bride. She had been, although she hadn't realised it at the time, a lonely, susceptible and unusually naïve eighteen-year-old who had fallen in love with a good-looking braggart who had never had anything in mind but adding a notch to his score of easy blonde tourists.

No one, except girls who had been through the same thing, could imagine the agony of remorse and anxiety which had been her retribution for two afternoons of disappointing lovemaking.

Looking back, she could not understand how Diego had managed to persuade her to repeat the experience when the first time had been such a disaster.

Not realising she was a virgin, he had assumed, that, like all other foreign girls he had known, she had no fear of pregnancy. When he found out this wasn't the case, he had managed to convince her, first, that it had been a disaster only because it was the first time for her;

and, secondly, that, by a lucky chance, it had happened at a time when she had nothing to worry about.

But when her second experience had ended in tears of disappointment and been followed by a sleepless night in case she *had* cause for worry, she had enough sense to know that she couldn't continue.

Whether his black-eyed charm might have overcome her resistance when she met him again, to say goodbye, she would never know. But Diego had arrived at their rendezvous on the back of a friend's motor-bike, his own machine being under repair. As he stepped off the pillion, the rider, not knowing she spoke Spanish, had looked her up and down and remarked that, even if she wasn't hot stuff like the girl at the disco the night before, she wasn't a bad-looking *chica* and he wouldn't mind taking over when Diego had had enough of her.

Now, lying in the comfortable visitors' bedroom in the flat of the man she had promised to marry, Diana relived that moment of soul-shrivelling humiliation.

It had been many months before she had recovered her self-respect. Even when she had been able to listen to the voice of common sense which told her that everyone made mistakes in life, and hers had hurt no one but herself, the memory of her total failure to derive even the smallest pleasure from the act of love had remained on the fringe of her consciousness, like a distant dark cloud, still far off but perhaps bringing a storm later on.

Tonight she had tried to tell Reid about this flaw in her nature. But, far from helping her to overcome her diffidence at discussing it with him, he had glossed it over, preferring to prove—as he thought—that with him she would have no problem.

But she knew in her bones that, although she could respond to his kisses and perhaps to limited love-play, when it came to making love fully, she would feel only shrinking distaste for what she had once imagined to be the most sublime pleasure in life.

For others, presumably, it was. But not for her.

When they went to see Lady Marriott the following day, Diana's engagement ring finger was adorned by a twisted band of three-colour gold encrusted with emeralds and diamonds.

When Reid had picked it out from a selection of beautiful rings, the jeweller had remarked that the design had been inspired by the jewels of the Italian Renaissance.

Sensing that her fiancé, as he was now, preferred it to any of the others she had tried on, Diana had said that she liked it best. Actually she would have been happier with a much less valuable ring. Although it would be insured, the knowledge that it could not be worth less than ten thousand pounds—perhaps more—was more of a worry than a joy. Particularly as the ring did not symbolise any tender emotions but only a coming together of recent wealth and ancient tradition.

Her mother was delighted with their news. She had never been anything but courageous and cheerful, but this seemed to give her a boost which had been lacking before.

During the first three weeks of their engagement, Reid spent most of his evenings with Diana, sometimes taking her out, sometimes watching television or listening to records.

Always his goodnight embrace was a matter of two or three minutes of holding her in his arms and kissing her. But he never went any further and, after a while, she began to stop wondering if he would, and to accept that, for reasons of his own, he wasn't going to make love to her until they were married.

Several times it crossed her mind that the reason his ardour never got out of hand could be that he was still carrying on a discreet liaison with another woman. It was seldom very late when he said goodnight. It was possible that he went from her arms to someone else's.

Whether or not there was any basis for that supposition, she could not deny that in general he took considerable trouble to behave as if their relationship was that of a normal couple.

He sent her flowers and brought her pretty boxes of hand-made chocolates and small surprise presents which had caught his eye on his way about London. He seemed to want to know everything which had happened to her before he knew her, except about her love affair. That was something he never referred to.

One night, after she had cooked a meal for him at the flat, they were watching a television programme when he moved from the other end of the sofa to sit beside her with his arm round her shoulders.

By this time Diana had become sufficiently at ease with him not to tense at every companionable gesture on his part. Being interested in the programme, she didn't even glance at him, but accepted his nearness with less reaction than if Bertie had come to settle himself at her feet.

But as soon as the programme was over, Reid used the remote control gadget to switch off the set and turned her face up to his for a kiss which did not alarm her until she heard a soft click and realised he had reached out a long arm to turn off the table lamp.

She opened her eyes and freed her lips.

'Why have you turned off the light?'

'To save power.'

Although she couldn't see his expression, his tone told her it was amused.

Then his mouth reclaimed hers and he continued to kiss her until her instinctive protest was dissolved by a stronger instinct to relax and respond to the warm persuasion of his lips.

Somehow, being in darkness seemed to sharpen all her other senses. She was intensely aware of the pleasant taste of his mouth, the clean natural scent of his skin, the softness of his cashmere jersey in contrast to the hard feel of his shoulders as her hands slipped up round his neck.

She had always known he was strong. One had only to look at him to see that. Now she could feel the latent power of his tall frame and muscular flesh in close contact with her own healthy young body. Fit as she was, she knew she would be no match for him if ever he chose to exert his formidable strength against her.

But civilised men didn't use brute strength against women—unless they were pushed beyond the limits of their control—and Reid's masterful but not ungentle hold on her had none of the indications that he might be becoming too ardent.

She slid a hand over his hair, which was coarser and crisper than her own. Everything about him was different, from the slightly rough texture of his cheek under her exploring fingertips to the angular line of his jaw where her own was rounded.

Presently, with a murmured, 'Wait a moment,' he stopped kissing her and drew away.

She wondered what he was doing until he took her in his arms again, and she found he had stripped off his jersey and was now clad only in his shirt. But she didn't realise he had unbuttoned it until, several minutes later, he captured one of her hands and put it inside his shirt, holding her palm against his chest so that she could feel the heat of his skin and the beating of his heart.

Diana gave a stifled gasp and tried to draw her hand free. But Reid wouldn't release it, holding it securely in place with his larger hand while his lips became more demanding.

She knew that she ought to stop him before things got out of hand. But somehow, drugged by his kisses, it was difficult to muster the will-power to push him firmly away from her. Now, instead of imprisoning her hand, he was deftly unfastening her blouse, pushing the straps of her bra off her shoulders, peeling away the satin and lace to explore and caress her small breasts.

It was madness, and Diana knew it, to allow him to touch her like this. But the gentle movements of his fingers made her quiver with delicious sensations. As he kissed a slow path down her neck, she gave a murmur of pleasure and her slim body writhed in his arms, not in an effort to escape but in an involuntary response to the feelings induced by his fondling.

Even when his mouth reached her breasts, she

couldn't bring herself to end it. All the voluptuous longings which she had repressed and ignored for the past two years were rising to the surface; and the clamour for release of her starved senses was more powerful than her inhibitions.

But when his hand touched her knee and moved lightly up her bare leg, it ignited a swift blaze of panic which had her fighting to free herself with a violence which took him by surprise so that, within seconds, she was out of his arms and on her feet.

She was arranging her bra when he switched on the lamp, making her shy from its light like a nervous creature of the night. A deep blush swept her face and throat.

Reid rose and captured her hands as they fumbled, trembling, with her buttons.

'What's the matter, Diana? We are engaged to be married,' he said mildly.

'That doesn't give you the right to make love to me if I don't want to,' she said angrily.

It was herself she was angry with, not him.

'Of course not, but you were giving me the impression that you did want to.'

'I—I got carried away. I'm sorry, I didn't mean to lead you on.'

'You didn't. I was leading you on.'

Her eyes were downcast. She couldn't bring herself to look up at him. But he sounded more amused than annoyed.

He said, 'I was hoping to spend the night with you. It's not unusual, you know.'

'Perhaps not ... but I'd rather wait.'

She attempted to free her hands, but he wouldn't release them, and she was uncomfortably conscious of her gaping shirt.

'Why?' he asked.

'Why?' she echoed blankly, taken aback at being expected to explain herself.

'Yes—why? A few minutes ago you were enjoying what was happening. What made you decide you must stop doing what Nature intended when she gave you a beautiful body?'

'I—I just think it's wrong,' she said lamely.

She couldn't begin to explain the real reason. It was altogether too complex; a combination of fears, none of which would make sense to him.

'If you were younger I would agree,' he conceded. 'But we're both responsible adults. How can it be wrong for us to make love if we want to?'

'I don't want to,' she reiterated vehemently.

'You're lying, my lovely,' he told her. 'You may feel you shouldn't want to, but that's a different thing from not wanting. I want to take you to bed, and you want to come with me. Deny me, and yourself, that pleasure if you feel you must. But don't deny the desire. That's deluding yourself, which is never a good thing.'

He let go of her hands and began to fasten her buttons for her. His own shirt, open to the waist, revealed a smooth, brown-skinned chest as muscular as a boxer's.

Diana averted her eyes, knowing that what he had said was true—or had been right up to the moment when his hand on her thigh had set off that strident mental alarm bell.

Reid turned away to retrieve his discarded jersey. As he put his arms into the sleeves and pulled the rest over his head, he said, 'I'm flying to Edinburgh tomorrow and it's possible I'll stay there overnight. If so, I'll call you during the evening, and see you the day after tomorrow. Goodnight, Diana.'

'You're going . . . already.' It was much earlier than the time when he usually left her.

'If I stay, we shall end up in bed together, and you don't want that. It's better for me to leave.' He patted her cheek, and moved towards the door.

'Reid——'

As she said his name, he checked his stride and lifted an enquiring eyebrow.

'Are you angry with me?' she asked, with a troubled expression.

He shook his head. 'I think you're being rather silly, but I've never been in favour of persuading women to make love against their better judgment, and I'm not going to start with my future wife.'

An hour later, by which time she was in bed, Diana was unable to concentrate on the book she was attempting to read because of the erotic feelings which Reid had aroused in her, and which had not yet subsided.

If she felt like this, how must he feel? Somehow she couldn't see Reid, in the grip of unsatisfied desire, retiring with a book. He was much more likely to seek out one of his former girl-friends who would need no persuasion to welcome him into her bed.

Probably it was the knowledge that it wouldn't be difficult for him to find someone more compliant which had made him accept her refusal good-temperedly; not going off in a huff as Diego had done when, at first, she had refused him.

Thinking about why she had panicked, she knew the basic reason was the simple fear of being hurt again. Believing, as he had told her later, that her reluctance had been merely to tease him, Diego had taken her roughly and painfully. With hindsight, she thought it probable that, even if he had loved her, he would have been a clumsy, selfish partner.

Because of her own experience—admittedly very limited—and the remark made by her mother about her disappointment, she was beginning to suspect that men who were wonderful lovers were few and far between. And if Reid, for all his experience, was as brutal as Diego, it was better not to know it beforehand, or she might get cold feet and be unable to go through with their marriage.

The fact that she had responded to his kisses and caresses this evening proved nothing. She had enjoyed kissing Diego. It had been the last act of love which had been such a cruel anticlimax, making her weep from disappointment as much as from being hurt.

If that was going to happen again, with Reid; or if there was some fault in her nature which would make it impossible for her ever to enjoy that side of marriage, it was better not to find it out until it was too late to back out.

A little less than two months after the operation, Patience's doctors let her return to an ordinary room and receive unmasked visitors.

'It's so lovely to see your faces again, my dears,' she said happily to Reid and Diana when, for the first time since the transplant, they were allowed in without masks, gowns and shoe covers. 'If all goes well, it won't be too much longer before they let me out of here. Only three or four weeks, perhaps. Meanwhile, I've had a brainwave.'

'Well, don't keep us in suspense,' said Diana, smiling, as her mother paused for effect, looking smugly from one to the other.

'Actually, it's my surgeon's idea,' said Lady Marriott. 'I was talking to him about you, and how you were waiting for me to be discharged before you got married, and he said it would really be better for you to marry before that. Then you could go off on your honeymoon, knowing that I was being well looked after. Whereas if I was at home, you might worry about me. And then he suggested that it would be possible to have a quiet family wedding here, in the hospital chapel, by special licence.'

Diana could hardly hide her dismay.

Reid said, 'An excellent scheme. I have no desire for a big wedding and, as you have no close relations and very few friends in this country, presumably you and Diana won't wish for one either.'

Her mother said, 'I was married in a register office. Women who miss having a traditional white wedding are supposed to try to make up for it by dragooning their daughters into having one, whether they want it or not. But unless, as you say, there are a host of friends and relations whose feelings would be hurt by being excluded, I see little point in going to a great deal of expense over a ceremony which is always memorable to the bridal couple, whatever form it takes. However, it is Diana's wedding, and her wishes are more important than mine.'

'I certainly don't want an elaborate wedding,' Diana agreed. 'But——'

She didn't know how to express her reluctance to advance the ceremoney when the reasons put forward by Mr Carter were so eminently sound.

'But what?' enquired Reid, arching an eyebrow. 'There's nothing to stop you having a pretty dress and a bouquet and so on, if that's what's bothering you.'

'No, no—of course not, darling,' agreed her mother. 'If you were to be married next week, it would mean buying a dress off the peg rather than having one made. But with your figure that's no problem.'

'I wasn't thinking about that. My dress is the least important thing,' said Diana. 'I . . . it was just that I'd visualised being married in the chapel at home . . . when you were completely recovered, Mummy. A hospital chapel seems such a sad place to be married in,' she went on, rather desperately. 'I mean, surely people only go there to pray during operations and when patients are critically ill? It isn't used for christenings and weddings, and harvest festivals and carol services . . . all the happy occasions which take place in most churches and chapels.'

'Let's go and have a look at it . . . see what sort of atmosphere it has,' suggested Reid. He stood up. 'We shan't be long, Lady M, and then we'll come and report back.'

The nurse on duty at the enquiry desk gave them directions for finding the chapel which, by staircase and corridor, was about five minutes' walk from her mother's room.

The chapel was empty when they arrived there. Architecturally, it was not to be compared with the fourteenth-century nuns' chapel at Mirefleur Abbey.

This was merely a large, lofty room lit by plain-glass clerestory windows and furnished and carpeted in shades of soft blue.

What immediately caught the eye, however, were two beautiful arrangements of flowers on either side of the altar. Later, Diana learned that these were the work of the wife of a distinguished consultant. She arranged them at her home outside London and had them delivered to the hospital by her husband's chauffeur. Their freshness, and the unusual variety of flower and foliage which composed them, redeemed the chapel from dullness, and brought to it some of the tranquillity of a country garden.

'This doesn't strike me as depressing. Should you dislike being married here?' Reid asked her, in a lowered voice.

If only she could answer honestly: say, I shouldn't mind where we were married if I loved you, and you loved me. But we don't, and I'm terrified it will be a fiasco—especially the sex part.

But because there was no love between them, the truth was impossible to utter. They were not on those terms She could only go on prevaricating.

'No, it's nicer than I imagined, but I wonder if Mummy is really equal to the excitement?'

'Her surgeon must think so, or he wouldn't have suggested it. With regard to our honeymoon, I feel that instead of going away we might be better advised to stay at the Abbey. August isn't a month in which anyone would choose to go abroad if their plans weren't governed by school holidays, and whether the weather is good or bad we can find plenty to occupy us there in deciding what needs to be done to the house and grounds. I think a great many couples would enjoy their wedding trip more at the end of their first year together, rather than at the start of their married life.'

This was a suggestion to which Diana could accede more readily. To be on home ground, as it were, was bound to make the honeymoon less of a strain than if it were spent in unfamiliar surroundings. And, as Reid said, planning the future of the estate would be a help in getting through the first difficult week or two of being husband and wife.

'I think that's a very good idea. I should much rather stay at home,' she agreed.

'In that case you'd better start looking for a wedding dress at once. It won't take long to make the other arrangements. Presumably the hospital has a chaplain. He could do the deed for us—unless you feel that your local vicar should be asked to officiate, or at least to assist.'

'I don't know. We'd better ask Mummy about that. I think to have two clergymen at such a small wedding would be rather absurd.'

Diana found her wedding dress at Caroline Charles, a designer with a more illustrious client of the same name. It was a dress she could wear on many future occasions, being made of coin-dotted voile with an unlined jacket with a large Puritan collar to go over the low-cut, tight-waisted bodice. The collar was of white organza. The voile was palest dove grey.

For her hat she went to the Princess of Wales's milliner, John Boyd, taking the dress for him to see and explaining about the special licence and the lack of time.

Two days later her hat was delivered; a small dove grey cap trimmed with a single white ostrich feather to curl against her cheek.

By then she had bought her shoes which were plain grey suede pumps with medium heels, and a very small matching clutch purse, just large enough to hold a lipstick and a handkerchief.

The evening before their wedding, she went with Reid to the airport to meet his mother and stepfather who were going to make use of the flat for a few days after the wedding.

As she had it fixed in her mind that his mother would be an Italian counterpart of Mrs Lane, with a tight

new perm for the occasion and very likely dressed in
black, Diana was startled to find that her future
mother-in-law was a highly sophisticated woman. She
was dressed partly in black, but only to the extent
of wearing a black silk raincoat lined with black
mink. Beneath this extremely undowdy outer garment
was a two-piece of fine jersey wool in a subtle
combination of colours which proclaimed it to be a
Missoni.

The delicious scent which wafted over Diana as the
Italian embraced her was probably Missoni's Frag-
rance.

'I've been in a fever of curiosity to see what sort of
girl has at last captivated my son,' was her opening
remark. 'And you see I was right, my dear Guido'—
speaking to the man beside her. 'I said it would be
someone like this—very young, very fresh, and yet with
a firm little chin which suggests that my arrogant son
won't have *everything* his own way. I'm delighted to
meet you, Diana. It's time Reid was married and settled
down. I don't want my grandchildren to remember me
only as an old lady in her dotage.'

Reid then produced another surprise by formally
introducing his stepfather as the Conte di Voturino,
which meant that his mother must now be a *contessa*.

The attractive man she had remarried at once
insisted that Diana must use his first name; and,
while mother and son fell into a separate conversation,
he proceeded to make himself extremely charming to
her. But it was a charm which, she sensed, was based
on real warmth of temperament and was not in any
way spurious.

'Are you nervous?' he asked her presently. 'I was
nervous the night before my wedding. I was very much
older than Reid when I first took the plunge into
matrimony. No doubt he's told you our story? No?
Well, we were in love as young people—I more than
Maria at that time. Both our families had lost
everything during the war. We were really poor ...
short of food even. So when a prosperous Englishman

appeared on the scene, Maria's father preferred him to me as a suitor. Michael Lockwood was a very forceful character—as his son is—and I, at that age, was quite shy and diffident, and those are characteristics which do not appeal to young women. They want to be swept off their feet, is it not so?'

'Perhaps,' she agreed, somewhat doubtfully.

'Maria enjoyed it very much,' he confided, with a rueful grin. 'As I expect you have liked being swept off your feet by her son. But he is a much better man than his father, so I don't think you will regret it. You will be very happy together.'

'In what way is he different from his father?' she asked.

'In many ways. He has a broader intelligence. In matters of business his father was a genius, but his mind wasn't open to the other things life has to offer. He was what you call a rough diamond, and he never tried to polish himself. Reid, even if he hadn't benefited from the education his father could afford to give him, would always have been a more complete man. He likes music and art and good food . . . and many other things.'

Including beautiful women, Diana thought, with a pang.

In the car conversation became general. At the flat she was commandeered by Maria to help her unpack. Mrs Lane was not there that evening. They were dining round the corner at the Ritz.

'I've brought you some things for your trousseau because Italian underwear is so pretty. I hope you'll like the colours I've chosen,' said Maria, lifting the lid of the small suitcase and shaking out a pale primrose nightgown of chiffon and lace

Altogether the case contained five sets, each garment interleaved with tissue, of exquisite, hand-made lingerie; nighties with matching wrappers or dressing jackets, slips and half slips, bras and French knickers or bikini briefs.

Soon the cover on Reid's double bed was hidden by

swathes of diaphanous fondant-coloured fabrics. Diana was overwhelmed.

None of the sets was white, she noticed. Perhaps the Contessa had assumed that Diana herself would have bought a white nightgown to wear tomorrow night. Or perhaps she hadn't been sure that white would be appropriate now that many girls, even of her daughter-in-law's age, were not inexperienced when they married.

'I don't know how to thank you,' she said. 'They're lovely. How very kind of you!'

'I always wanted a daughter, but Reid's father wanted one son and then no more children. He had been part of a large family himself, and he hadn't liked it. As soon as he could, he cut himself off from them.'

The Contessa began to unpack the larger suitcase containing her own clothes. She showed Diana her dress for the wedding. It was dark red, the colour of mulberries.

'You know, I have always felt guilty about leaving England when I did,' she said, as Diana handed her a padded hanger. 'Although Reid has never expressed any resentment about my separation from his father, as the years passed and he didn't marry I began to wonder if, subconsciously, he was afraid to give his heart to a girl because the first woman he loved—which was me— had deserted him.'

'But he wasn't a little boy when you left. When he told me about it, he seemed to feel you'd done the right thing. I don't think being afraid is in his nature,' said Diana.

'No, you are right, it isn't. If he were afraid, he would recognise the feeling and force himself to do the thing which frightened him,' agreed his mother. 'Now I know that he was merely waiting until the right girl came along. But we women are saddled with a great weight of tradition which makes us feel terribly guilty if we deviate from the accepted pattern of marriage and motherhood. I was torn between feeling that I ought to stay in England until Reid was at least eighteen, and fearing that, if I did, I might lose Guido for good. What an uncomfortable condition love is when there are problems! But once they are all resolved . . . ah, then it is worth all the heartaches.'

She changed the subject after that and enquired about Lady Marriott's progress and the arrangements for the wedding.

But much later that night, after they had strolled back from the hotel leaving Reid to spend his last night there, she came to Diana's bedroom for a preview of her wedding dress.

When she had admired it, she said, 'May I give you a little advice?'

'Of course . . . please do,' said Diana.

'Don't let Reid dominate you too much. He is a superb organiser, and will take over everything—even your dinner parties—if you let him. Try to resist that; to keep certain areas of your life under your control. I'm telling you this because it was the mistake I made with his father. I was a foreigner in a strange country, so naturally I turned to Michael for advice on many matters which I could have handled by myself in Italy. In the end, my first husband was not advising but dictating every aspect of my life—even to the kind of clothes I should wear.'

She smiled, and patted Diana's arm 'I don't say this will happen with you and Reid, because you are on your home ground. But it's a pitfall to be beware of. Brides are apt to think their husbands are perfect, but no human being is perfect. The people who understand that and come to terms with it are the ones whose marriages last. Now I must leave you to get your beauty sleep. Goodnight, my dear. Happy dreams!'

Next morning Diana received a special delivery from a Mayfair jeweller famous for fine antique pieces. The long narrow case contained a five-strand Edwardian pearl choker with a diamond and moonstone centre.

Since the present Princess of Wales had revived the

fashion set by her predecessor, the beautiful Danish princess who had later become Queen Alexandra, London had abounded with chokers ranging from inexpensive reproductions on the junk jewellery counters to very costly examples, some in their original form and some hurriedly-made adaptations of less modish lengths of pearls and currently unfashionable brooches.

As she lifted it from its velvet bed, and put it round her throat, Diana guessed that this particular choker had once belonged to an Edwardian society beauty who had worn it at the spectacular balls and dinner parties during King Edward VII's brief reign at the beginning of the century. Perhaps it had not been worn since then.

The card which had come with it bore no romantic message, but simply R.L. to D.H. and, beneath their initials, the date.

But the choker itself was a romantic choice, very much in fashion and yet with the nostalgic charm of its period. Probably it was more satisfactory to have a husband who gave one delightful presents without tender inscriptions, than one whose gifts were less well chosen but accompanied by loving words, she thought.

The guests at the wedding included Christopher Tarrant, who had visited Patience twice while she was still in isolation, and seemed likely to become a more frequent visitor in future.

Diana was given away by Lady Marriott's surgeon. His wife and the consultant's wife who did the flowers for the chapel and who, today, had excelled herself, were among the small congregation who were present at the ceremony and afterwards attended the informal wedding breakfast held in the hospital's boardroom.

If, as several people told her, Diana looked radiant, it was largely from the joy she felt at seeing her mother transformed from the tired, breathless, haggard woman she had been when they landed in England to

someone with bright, smiling eyes who already looked
much too well to be confined to a wheelchair.

Her daughter's delight on that score was reflected in
another face. Ratclyffe, who had come up by train the
previous day but was returning by road with the bride
and groom, could hardly take his eyes off Lady
Marriott.

Although Diana had been home to see him and
Bertie several times in recent weeks, today she was
struck by how much he had aged since their arrival at
the Abbey. Then she had been astonished to learn how
old he was. Now there was a frailness about him which
made her think it should be a matter of priority to
engage other staff and insist that Ratty should take life
more easily.

There was plenty of room for him to have
comfortable quarters where he could live out his
retirement in the surroundings he loved, perhaps
continuing to take a minor part in the running of the
household.

She was glad when the formalities were over.
Although people tended to see what they expected to
see—obviously everyone thought her a very lucky girl
to have such a tall, personable bridegroom—it was still
a strain trying to look as if this were the happiest day of
her life.

It was not without its satisfactions—she had freed
her mother from financial worries and secured the
future of the Abbey as a family house—but her
wedding night, and all the nights after it, gave her
shivers in the pit of her stomach if she allowed herself
to think about it.

'Goodbye, my dears. This has been *such* a happy day
for me,' said Patience, when the time came for them to
take leave of her. 'I always hoped Diana would find
someone like you to take care of her, and make up for
her unsettled childhood. I know you will do that par
excellence, Reid. I couldn't wish for a kinder son-in-
law.'

He bent to kiss her cheek. 'I won't keep her away

from you too long.'

'Now I shall be very cross if you curtail your honeymoon on my account. Diana can telephone me from time to time, but I don't want you hurrying back to London because of me. In the lovely weather which is forecast, the country is the place to be. The next time I see you, darling'—this to her daughter—'I shall expect you to be as brown as you used to be in Spain. Make her sunbathe every day, Reid. Begin as you mean to go on, and take a very firm line with her.'

This was said as a joke, and Reid grinned. 'Don't worry—I mean to,' he answered, as he took his bride's hand in his.

They had been asked by the Chief Nursing Officer if they would object to doing a brief tour of the wards before leaving the hospital. In spite of Reid's wish to avoid all publicity, the story of their wedding had leaked out and received a good deal of press coverage. But even if it had not done so, everyone in the hospital would have known about it, for word had spread among the nurses and among the auxiliary staff who attended to all the non-medical duties.

Later in the day, all the patients who were not on restricted diets would be given a piece of wedding cake with their four o'clock tea; and, although Diana didn't know this until she was told by the Sister in charge of the first ward they went to, Reid had arranged for every patient to receive a beautiful posy of summer flowers in celebration of the occasion. These had been delivered that morning and had obviously given a great deal of pleasure, especially as the posies were contained in small crystal vases which would be a permanent memento. She learned, too, that almost everyone had had champagne with their lunch.

As she and her husband made their way along the wards—and it took much longer than they had anticipated because everyone wanted to thank them and wish them well—there were times when she was touched almost to tears by the warmth of these strangers' good wishes, and the women's delight in her dress and the ostrich-feathered hat.

She could see in their faces that, somehow, on this special day, she and Reid personified everyone's dream of love in full flower; a dream which did not lose its magic even for people whose own marriages had not worked out as well as they had hoped.

It was a moving experience to feel herself representing an ideal of happiness to them; and an uplifting one, too. By the time it was over, she had begun to feel that perhaps, if she worked at it hard enough, she could translate the dream into reality and make Reid love her and she him.

They drove out of London in his car, with Ratty in the back with a hamper from Fortnum & Mason containing a cold collation for their supper that night and lunch tomorrow.

Bertie had been left overnight with one of Ratty's cronies in the village. When they arrived there to collect the dog, they found quite a large crowd of women, children, and old men waiting to see them.

At the Abbey, it was Reid who carried their cases up to the bedroom which from now on they would share. Like the principal bedrooms in all aristocratic houses, it had an adjoining dressing-room for his use, and a boudoir for hers. Soon these were to be converted into spacious bathrooms, but meanwhile they were as they had always been. So far, only the mattress on the bed had been changed for a new one specially made to the bed's large dimensions.

As they mounted the ancient staircase, Diana was reminded of her first day at the Abbey when Reid had taken her own and her mother's luggage upstairs for them. Little had she dreamed, that afternoon, that soon she would be Mrs Reid Lockwood.

'Shall we take Bertie for a walk and stretch our own legs at the same time?' he suggested.

'Yes, I'd like a walk,' she agreed.

He began to loosen the knot of his tie. As she took off her grey voile jacket and he saw the tight-waisted dress beneath it, he asked, 'Do you need unzipping?'

The tag of the zip, being level with the bottom of her shoulderblades, was not a difficult one to reach. But she felt she ought to say, 'Yes please,' and turn her back.

Then she wondered if, having undone the zipper, he would decide to continue helping her to undress and to forget about the walk, and she wished she had refused the offer. She didn't want to be made love to in daylight, and she thought it would help her to relax if she had several glasses of wine with her supper.

However, having opened the zip, Reid made no attempt to assist her to remove the dress, but went on with his own undressing.

Wondering if he were watching her, Diana stepped out of the dress which, being lined with silk, had not needed a petticoat or half-slip. Her only underpinnings were a bra, bikini briefs and a suspender belt to hold up her almost invisibly sheer stockings.

Knowing that bare thighs above stocking tops were supposed to have an inflammatory effect on men, but not knowing how true this was, as she bent over her suitcase to unpack a sun-dress, she would not have been surprised to feel his hands on her hips.

But as she shook out the dress and shot a furtive glance at him, he was standing several yards away from her, in the act of shrugging off his shirt.

She had never seen him bare-shouldered before and the sight of him stripped to the waist, his broad shoulders tapering to a midriff with no superfluous flesh around it, and his upper arms bulging with muscle, made her give a slight gasp of surprise. She had known he was lean and powerful, but she had not guessed it would be she who would feel a tingle of excitement at the sight of his half-naked body.

Quickly she put on her dress and did up the buttons before lifting the skirt to unclip her stockings and peel them off.

'You have very nice legs,' said Reid.

She glanced up to find him standing in his underpants, putting the bottoms of his trousers together. His own legs were long and slim, not very hairy.

'In fact you have very nice everything,' he added.

She had the feeling that, although she hadn't seen him looking at her while she was in her underwear, he had looked and approved of the body which, later, he would see in its entirety.

She found herself blushing. 'Thank you.'

He smiled at her. 'There's nothing to be nervous about, Diana.'

'I—I know. I'm not,' she assured him, untruthfully.

The fact that, just for a second, she had admired his strength and symmetry did not mean she wasn't dreading the moment when those powerful arms would draw her to him.

One could admire the rippling sinews of a panther. But to be in a cage with a panther . . .

'I think you are—a little,' he said mildly. He had put on some other trousers now. Having pulled up the zip, he strolled towards her. Taking her chin in his hand, he tilted her face up to his. But he only kissed the tip of her nose, not her quivering lips.

'Don't be,' he admonished. 'It isn't necessary.'

They took Bertie for a long walk in the summer woods.

'How quiet it is here. I'd forgotten,' Diana said, after they had been walking in silence for some time, each preoccupied with their own thoughts.

'Yes, your mother was right—this is the best place to be at this time of year, in fine weather. Better than Greece or Italy which will both be swarming with tourists. We'll go there. We'll go everywhere. But for peace and privacy in August, nowhere can touch this corner of England,' said Reid.

They had tea on the terrace. When Ratty asked what time they wanted to dine, her husband said, 'At seven-thirty.'

As by then it was nearly six o'clock, Diana went up to have a bath and to change into something more glamorous than the rather faded blue sun-dress she had put on to walk in the woods.

The scent of roses and honeysuckle drifted up through the open windows as she brushed her hair and debated what to wear for supper. Ratty had finished their unpacking for them while they were out. All their clothes had been put away, and the cases removed.

She was dressed in a long green robe with loose sleeves and a deep V neck when Reid came in.

'I've been poking about in the attics and I'm covered in dust. I need a bath. Bring me a drink, will you, sweetie. I asked Ratty to bring up a drinks tray.'

'What sort of drink would you like?'

'Gin. Ice. A slice of lemon. Tonic.' He headed for the bathroom.

When she took the drink to him, he was lounging in the boxed-in bath which, though deep, was too short for his height. The water came up to his armpits, but his raised knees broke the surface like islands.

'Thanks. Put it on here, would you?' He tapped the wide ledge of varnished mahogany which surrounded the rim of the bath. 'Do you ever have a drink in your bath?'

'Not so far. Mummy used to sometimes. A glass of white wine in a cool bath on a hot night. I always had showers in Spain, although I've had baths at your flat.'

As she spoke, she avoided looking at him. But she was intensely aware of the long, relaxed, masculine body lying at ease in the still steaming water.

'I'll go down and help Ratty,' she said.

'Yes, do. The old boy looks tired. Before you go, there's one more thing you can give me.'

'Yes—what is it?'

'A kiss.'

He reached out an arm and encircled her wrist with

his fingers, forcing her to lean down to him.

To stop herself overbalancing, she had to put her free hand on his shoulders. It felt warm and solid under her palm. His mouth, too, was warm against hers, and this time the kiss wasn't brief. It seemed to go on for ever, and she didn't know whether it was the kiss or being bent over the bath which made her feel dizzy.

At last he released her mouth, but without letting go of her wrist. Smiling at her bemused expression, he said, 'It's a pity you had your bath earlier. We could have had one together. No—I think you're too shy at the moment. We'll reserve that pleasure for next week.'

Then he laughed and let her go, and she bolted out of the bathroom with flaming cheeks and a wildly accelerated heartbeat.

By the time Reid came down to supper she had recovered her composure. They ate in the sunset glow of a perfect evening at a table by the library window. Diana did her best to enjoy the delicious things which he had ordered for this luxurious indoor picnic, but her appetite seemed to have deserted her.

At the end of the meal, when they had been waiting for some time for Ratty to bring their coffee, she went to the kitchen to see what was delaying him.

The butler was sitting in his chair at the side of the Aga. It wasn't the first time that she had discovered him having forty winks. He was, after all, an old man who in normal circumstances would have retired long ago instead of continuing to serve his eccentric employer and, recently, his daughter and granddaughter.

Suddenly, as she looked at his slumped form, his white head turned to one side against the old-fashioned antimacassar, something in the way his hands hung over the sides of the chair instead of being clasped and resting on his waistcoat, as they usually were when he was snoozing, sent a thrill of apprehension through her.

'Ratty?' she said uncertainly.

He didn't stir. Ordinarily, when he was napping, the slightest sound was enough to rouse him.

'Ratty . . . are you all right?'

But even as she hurried across the kitchen, she knew in her bones what had happened.

His right hand, when she took it in hers, was warm. But her touch did not make him awaken, blinking, momentarily disorentated. There was no pulse to be felt in his thin old wrist, no blood coursing through the prominent blue veins in the white skin.

She placed the lax hand in his lap.

'Oh, Ratty . . .' she whispered aloud, moving round to do the same with the other.

From that side she could see him full face. His lower jaw had dropped as it did when he was dozing. There was nothing in his expression to suggest that he had felt unwell. He appeared to have sat down to rest, and his long life had come to an end as if he had fallen asleep.

For him, Diana was glad. For herself, she felt a sharp grief at the loss of a newly-made friend, someone infinitely trustworthy and kind and, in character, a much finer person than the selfish, irascible old man who had been her grandfather.

She went back to the library to tell Reid. There were tears in her eyes as she said, 'Reid, can you come? Ratty is dead.'

He sprang up, saying, 'Are you sure? Where is he?'

'In the kitchen . . . in his chair.'

'It could be a stroke or a coronary.'

Leaving her to follow, he tore out of the room. She had never seen him move so fast.

When she returned to the kitchen, he was gently closing the old man's eyes.

'No, you're right. He is dead,' he said gravely. 'If you'll show me where it is, I'll carry him up to his room. Then we must call your local doctor.'

The butler's bedroom was not far from the kitchen.

In the days when the Abbey had had a full staff, it had been the housekeeper's room, next to the still-room.

As Diana would have expected, it was as immaculate as the old man himself had always been. Advancing years had not made Ratty lapse into slovenliness as elderly people sometimes did. The strict disciplines of his early years in service had remained with him to the end.

Reid, who had carried his limp form without any difficulty, laid him down on the clean white bedspread and folded his arms.

'I think he would have wanted his shoes to be taken off,' she said huskily.

He did as she suggested, revealing neat darns in the toes of the butler's socks.

'Was the local doctor treating him for anything, do you know?' he asked.

'I don't think so. I don't think Ratty had anything the matter with him. If he did, he never mentioned it.'

'In that case it's important for the doctor to examine him immediately. Otherwise he may have to notify the coroner. What's the doctor's name?'

'Lawrence. You met his son and daughter one day at The Nun's Head.'

'Oh, yes, I remember.' He put his arm round her shoulder and steered her from the room.

Within ten minutes of Reid's telephone call to him, Dr Lawrence arrived at the Abbey.

'It's very unfortunate that this should have happened today of all days,' he said, when he and Reid had rejoined her in the library, and he was making out the medical certificate. 'Try not to let it upset you, Diana. A quick, quiet end at his age is a good way to die.'

'I know,' she agreed, her throat tight. 'But he was such a dear. It would have been nice if he could have lived to see everything running smoothly again.'

'I'm sure it made him very happy to be at your wedding today, and to know that the future of the Abbey was in such capable hands.'

He gave the certificate to Reid and asked if he had dealt with a similar situation before.

'Yes, I arranged my father's funeral. I can handle this for Diana. Will you have a nightcap with us, Doctor Lawrence?'

The doctor thanked him but refused. 'If there's any way in which I can be of assistance, don't hesitate to telephone.' He turned to Diana. 'Don't allow this to cast a shadow on your honeymoon, my dear. Ratclyffe wouldn't have wished you to grieve for him.'

She nodded. 'Thank you for coming. Goodnight.'

When the two men had left the room, she sat down, striving to contain her emotions. It wasn't fair to Reid to give way to tears on her wedding night. He had liked the old man, but he hadn't been fond of him.

When Bertie came and laid his black muzzle on her lap, and looked up at her with an expression in his soft brown eyes which seemed to say, 'What's wrong? Why are you unhappy? Can't I comfort you?' it was too much for her control.

As she bent to fondle his velvety ears, her eyes brimmed and overflowed. A bright drop fell on his fur.

When Reid returned from seeing the doctor to his car, he found her crouched on the hearthrug, her arms round the dog, her slim shoulders shaking with sobs which, even in her distress, she knew were not wholly for Ratclyffe. They were also, in part, for herself, because today she had been a bride, but with little of the eager joy a bride ought to feel on her wedding day.

Whatever impatience he felt inwardly, Reid didn't remonstrate with her. He drew her to her feet and would have let her cry on his shoulder if she hadn't, by a great effort, pulled herself together.

'I'm sorry. I'm b-better now,' she murmured, in an unsteady voice. 'Could I borrow your handkerchief, please?'

He gave it to her, still keeping his arms lightly round her while she dried her eyes.

'Shall I make coffee now?' she asked.

'What you need is a sedative, not a stimulant. Do you dislike hot milk?'

'Yes, I can't bear the skin.'

'I'll have a look round to see if there's any cocoa or chocolate. You go up and get ready for bed.'

'What about Bertie? His basket is in Ratty's room, but I don't think he should sleep there tonight. He's too intelligent not to know something is wrong.'

'He can sleep with me in the dressing-room, although I think later we should train him to sleep in the hall,' he replied.

She gave him an uncertain glance. 'The dressing-room?'

He said, 'You're exhausted, my dear. It's been a strenuous day for you, apart from a sad shock this evening. We're going to be married a long time. We don't have to start sleeping together tonight. Tomorrow is another day. Off you go. In a few minutes I'll bring you something to help you to nod off.'

Could he tell what a flood of relief she experienced at this unlooked-for reprieve from the ordeal of being made his wife in fact as well as law? She hoped not.

Not that Reid seemed the kind of man who would be put off by his bride's lack of eagerness to consummate their union. Probably he was confident he could overcome her reluctance.

'All right ... thank you,' she said, in a low tone. 'Shall I take Bertie up with me now?'

'Yes, do. I'll bring his basket up presently.'

As she went up the stairs to what, after tonight, would be their bedroom, she did not care that this was only a postponement of the moment she dreaded; the moment when he would claim his right to enjoy her unwilling body.

At least she was spared that tonight. As he had realised, she was exhausted. There was no way she could have simulated the responses to which he was entitled.

Before going to the bathroom, she went to the walk-in linen cupboard and found sheets and pillowcases with which to make up the single bed in the dressing-room. She hoped they and the bed were not damp. She wouldn't like Reid to have his forbearance rewarded with a chill. However, both the linen and the mattress felt dry.

Mindful that it wouldn't be long before he came up, she confined her preparations for bed to quickly creaming off her make-up and brushing her teeth.

When her husband entered the bedroom, she was sitting up on one side of the imposing bed, her diaphanous nightdress concealed by a frilly dressing jacket.

'I found a tin of Ovaltine. You may not like the stuff, but drink as much as you can,' said Reid. 'I should have asked Lawrence for a couple of mild sleeping pills for you.'

Without stopping to think, Diana said, 'Wouldn't he have thought that very odd ... sleeping pills on our wedding night?'

'I daresay not, in the circumstances. Anyway, what other people think is a matter of indifference to me. My concern is that you should sleep well.'

He had found a small round tray to hold the beaker of Ovaltine, and he put it on her lap.

'You're very kind. Thank you, Reid.'

'Didn't you expect me to be kind to you?' he asked, looking down at her with a rather enigmatic expression.

'Yes, of course, but——' She stopped.

It would not be tactful to tell him that, earlier in the day, she would not have thought there were any circumstances, short of the house burning down, which would have deflected him from taking her tonight.

'But with some reservations, it seems,' he said, in a dry tone. 'Well, I have many shortcomings, but breaking my word is not one of them. Having promised to cherish you, I shall strive to do so.'

But we also promised to love each other, and we both

knew *that* was a false promise, was the thought which came into her mind.

He stooped to kiss her on the forehead. 'Goodnight, Diana. Come along, Bertie.'

Snapping his fingers to signal the Labrador to follow him, Reid walked out of the room.

CHAPTER SIX

DIANA woke up to find the sun shining and her watch showing past nine o'clock. She had been asleep for the better part of twelve hours.

Although she was conscious of feeling rested, there was also a secondary awareness of something amiss. It was a feeling she had experienced regularly from the first diagnosis of her mother's illness until Patience was out of danger.

Now it was a few moments before she realised that today it was not the transplant but Ratty's death which oppressed her.

Was Reid still asleep in the next room?

Slipping out of bed, she padded to the dressing-room door and quietly opened it.

The bed in the corner had been made and Bertie's basket was empty.

It took her about twenty minutes to wash, dress and make her own bed. As she walked to the head of the staircase, she heard Reid's voice coming from below her. He was obviously making a telephone call.

He saw her coming down the staircase as he was replacing the receiver.

'Good morning. Sleep well?' he asked.

'Good morning. Yes, thank you. And you?'

He nodded. 'I was going to bring you breakfast in bed, but you've beaten me to it.'

'Who were you telephoning?'

'The undertakers suggested by Dr Lawrence. They'll come over this morning and do what's necessary. I thought you would rather the old man stayed here, in the chapel, than was taken away to their premises. We can have his funeral here, too. Where he's buried depends on whether he's left any instructions among his papers. There may also be relations to notify.'

'What about Mummy?' asked Diana. 'Must I tell her, do you think?'

'No, I shouldn't, for the time being. But I assume you'll call her every day to find out how things are with her? She's bound to feel rather bereft with her ewe lamb now a married woman.' He put an arm round her waist, and smiled at her. 'What would you like for breakfast, Mrs Lockwood?'

The organisation of Ratclyffe's funeral took up most of the day. Without Reid to guide her through the various formalities, Diana would have found it an onerous business.

He also made an arrangement for their evening meals to be brought to them from The Nun's Head until he could engage a cook and the nucleus of the staff needed to run the house properly.

That night when, about ten o'clock, Diana smothered a yawn, he said, 'I think another early night wouldn't do you any harm. I'm going to read for a while.'

For the second night in succession, she had the great bed to herself.

James William Ratclyffe was buried in the village churchyard on the fifth day of what purported to be their honeymoon.

By then Diana's relief had changed to bewilderment. When *was* Reid intending to join her in the bedroom? One could be forgiven for thinking that he had as little inclination to spend his nights with her as she had to share them with him.

The evening after the funeral, he said, 'I've arranged to borrow a pony which is used to drawing a small cart. Tomorrow we'll harness him to the trap in the coach-house and drive round the circuit.'

'You mean the boundaries?' asked Diana, thinking he must be referring to the lanes outside the high walls erected in the nineteenth century when labour and bricks were cheap enough for landowners to think nothing of having miles of wall erected.

'No, the circuit is something I was introduced to at school, and now I find you have one here.'

By this time she knew that he had been educated at Stowe, once the home of the Dukes of Buckingham, for the past sixty years, a boys' public school which one of its former pupils, film star David Niven, had described as 'the most beautiful school in England.' Unlike most of the country's famous schools with their much longer histories going back to the fourteenth and fifteenth centuries, Stowe School had come into being because the last aristocrat to own the great house—the Master of Kinloss—had been one of the millions of casualties in the first world war.

A few years later, in 1923, the property had been bought by a consortium who thought there was scope for a new public school. Recently, in speaking of his schooldays to her mother, Reid had quoted the first headmaster who—long before his time there—had said, 'Every boy who goes out from Stowe will know beauty when he sees it for the rest of his life'; this being a reference to the magnificence of the eighteenth-century house and the splendour of its grounds.

'The circuit is something which developed between about 1720 and 1780,' he explained. 'Before that, gardens and parks had always been laid out with the main lines converging on the house. Then they began to be planned in a circular style; the inner circle, not far from the house, being for walking, and the outer one for riding and driving. At Stowe there's a very famous circuit with stopping points at about thirty garden buildings. There's another at Stourhead in Wiltshire where the grounds are some of the finest in Europe. They have a Temple of Flora, a Chinese bridge, a rustic cottage, a pantheon—all sorts of features.'

'And we have the same thing here?' Diana asked, in surprise.

'On a modest scale, yes. But some of the path which used to link the points of interest seem to have disappeared. Come over here and I'll show you a plan of the grounds which I found when I was browsing in here last night after you'd gone up.'

He led her across the room to a large map table on which, in a huge portfolio, were a collection of architectural drawings. Reid turned them over until he came to the one he wanted.

'Look—d'you see?—There's the temple . . . the ice-house . . . the bath-house . . . the rotunda . . . and finally the grotto. In all, a drive of several miles. With stops, an afternoon's excursion.'

Diana leaned over the plan which, as well as the buildings he had indicated, showed the natural features of the estate as it had been two hundred years ago.

But what she was most aware of, as her gaze scanned the drawing, was of Reid's tall figure leaning over the table beside her. It was the closest they had been since he had lifted her, weeping, into his arms on their wedding night.

She wondered suddenly if he was expecting her to give him some kind of signal that she had recovered from the strain of the wedding and Ratty's death, and was ready to fulfil her obligations.

But the fact of the matter was that she wasn't and, deep in her heart, never would be. Sleeping with him, submitting herself to his lovemaking—if it could be called that when no love was involved on either side—was the price she must pay for retaining possession of the Abbey and having access to his fortune.

And yet, as she stood beside him and, out of the corner of her eye, saw one strong hand spread on the table—the hand which, sooner or later, would make free with her shrinking flesh—she felt that to postpone the inevitable could only aggravate the ordeal.

Better to get it over and done with. The first time would be much the worst. After a while she would get used to it . . . would have to get used to it.

'Were you very late last night?' she asked without looking up.

'Fairly late. There's so much fascinating stuff in here. I didn't disturb you when I did come up, did I?'

'No, I didn't hear a sound.'

'I tried not to make too much noise, but my light showing under the door might have woken you.'

'Nothing wakes me once I'm asleep.' She moved away from the table. 'Are you staying up late again tonight?'

Reid straightened, thrusting his hands into the pocket of his jeans.

'Possibly. Why do you ask?'

She found it impossible to meet his level gaze, or to find the words for what she wanted to convey.

'Well . . . I . . .' was as far as she got before he said quietly, 'Are you inviting me to spend the night with you, Diana?'

She felt herself turning bright scarlet. Her eyes on the floor, she said, her voice barely audible, 'If . . . if you want to.'

There was a pause before he moved towards her and tipped up her chin.

'Oh, I want to,' he said, in an odd tone, and with a strange light in his eyes. 'But I don't think you do—not yet. But you will . . . when the right moment comes.'

For an instant, she thought he was going to kiss her. Instead, he let go of her chin and strolled back to the chair where he had been sitting before.

'So, as I was saying, tomorrow we'll emulate your ancestors and go for a drive round the circuit,' he went on. 'Perhaps we'll make a picnic of it. The carriage I should like to have put in order is the phaeton. In their day, they were the equivalent of sports cars, you know.'

'Yes, so I believe.'

His attitude baffled her. When would the right moment come? If he knew that she wasn't eager to begin their sex life, what did he think was going to alter her attitude?

That night she *did* hear him come to bed in the adjoining room. For a long time after he had switched out his light, she lay awake in the darkness, wondering how many docile girls had, in this bed, submitted their bodies to an act which gave them no pleasure.

At mid-morning, with an elderly pony harnessed to the shafts of the trap, they set out on their tour of the park.

Reid had found a hoop of large keys which he hoped might unlock the buildings along the circuit. Their first stop was at the ice-house. It was built not far from the lake which had supplied the blocks of ice to be stored in it till the hot weather. But none of the keys on the ring fitted the lock on the door.

'And if one of them had, probably it wouldn't have turned,' he said with a shrug, before they walked back to the trap.

When Diana remarked on his expert handling of the reins, he laughed. 'A child could manage this little mare. Do you want to have a go?'

She shook her head. His good-humoured mood surprised her. She would have thought that after nearly a week of this curious travesty of a honeymoon, he would be becoming noticeably short-tempered. Instead he seemed in excellent spirits.

Perhaps his delight in his new property—for he was the master here now even if, for courtesy's sake, he continued to defer to her mother—counterbalanced her failure to delight him.

At the bath-house they had better luck. Here one of the keys did fit, and they heard the click of the lock opening. Even then the door would not open until Reid had put his shoulder to it and exerted considerable strength. Eventually, with a creaking of rusty hinges, it swung inwards.

The interior of the place, which was very dark, was like a small indoor swimming pool. It had changing rooms on both sides, and stone steps leading down to the floor of the deep oval pool.

'What I don't understand,' said Diana, 'is why they built it such a long way from the house.'

'Because it was probably only used once a week, if that. The cold bath was a health fad, not a place to get clean,' Reid explained. 'I wonder if we could adapt it into a jacuzzi. No, I think not. It's better left as it is . . . an interesting relic of the past.'

They had lunch in a sheltered glade not far from the rotunda. Earlier, Reid had been to the nearest market town, about nine miles away, where the shops included a good wine merchant and a delicatessen. But what he had put in the picnic basket Diana did not discover until she unpacked it.

She did this while he was unharnessing the amiable pony and tethering her by a long rope so that she could graze while they ate.

By the time he joined Diana, she had spread a cloth on the grass and set out the china and cutlery, and the containers of food. He had bought all kinds of good things, including rye bread, cottage cheese, an earthenware crock of pâté, some slices of Suffolk ham, and one of her favourite French cheeses, Boursin *au poivre*, which she liked for the spicy coating of crushed black peppercorns complementing the creamy interior.

This was not all he had provided, but it was all she had investigated when he joined her carrying a cool box.

This proved to contain several bottles. A few minutes later she was sipping ice-cold champagne, with a cuckoo calling from the depths of the beechwoods, and the scent of warm grass on the air.

'This is lovely, Reid,' she said, with a smile.

Even though she wasn't in love with him, she had to admit he was being extraordinarily nice to her. If only marriage didn't involve ... Her mind shied away from the memory of a garden in Spain, and a younger man's rough, clumsy hands, and her pain, and his heavy breathing.

'What with one thing and another, you haven't done much of the sunbathing your mother recommended,' said Reid, while they were finishing the meal with ripe, juicy greengages. 'Why don't you take off your dress?'

He had already taken off his shirt.

'Perhaps I will in a minute. Aren't these gorgeous?'— after biting into another greengage from one of the trees espaliered to the old red brick wall which surrounded the Abbey's kitchen garden.

A little later, he said, 'I'm going for a ramble. Want to come? Or would you prefer a siesta?'

'How can you be so energetic? I can't muster the energy to move!'

'Have a snooze, then, sweetie.'

He strolled off towards the dappled shadows of the woods.

There was still some champagne in her glass. She finished it slowly, in sips, knowing that if she had been anywhere but here, with anyone else but her husband, she would have stopped drinking two glasses ago.

When she stood up to take off her dress, she felt quite steady on her feet, but she also felt divinely carefree.

Presently, stretched out in the sun in her scanty underthings, she thought about the women who had lived at the Abbey before her, but who had never known this lovely sensation of golden warmth beaming down on—almost—bare skin. How uncomfortable they must have been in all those layers of petticoats and tight bodices, she thought drowsily.

She dreamt that she was among a party of people in

eighteenth-century clothes having a picnic. They weren't sitting on the grass but were seated round a long polished table, being waited on by several servants. Barney Lawrence was there, in a wig, and Val in a yellow silk gown and a hat tied under her chin with long yellow ribbons. Reid had on a red velvet coat with lace at his throat and wrists and his dark hair tied back with a bow. The flamboyant clothes only emphasised his masculinity; the strength of the hands emerging from the white lace ruffles, the breadth of the shoulders under the soft garnet velvet.

As she watched him, he beckoned her to him. She rose from her end of the table and went to him. Ignoring the rest of the party, he pulled her on to his lap and kissed her.

She was in his arms, kissing him back, when she realised it had stopped being a dream. The strong arms, the warm lips, were real.

Afterwards, she fell asleep again. When she woke up for the second time, she was aware, first, of being happy; then of being naked; and then of Reid lying beside her, propped up on one elbow, watching her.

He was nibbling a long stalk of grass which, as she gathered her wits—not sure if what she remembered had really happened or had been a wild, wonderful fantasy—he removed from between his white teeth.

Gently brushing the tip of her breast with the feathery tip of the grass, he said. 'Well, Mrs Lockwood—how now?'

She knew then that it hadn't been a figment of her imagination. Between her first and second nap, he had made long, heavenly love to her; making a nonsense of her belief that the heights of bliss were summits she would never climb.

'I feel marvellous,' she answered, lazily stretching herself.

His grey eyes glinted with amusement. 'You won't mind repeating the experience?'

She shook her head, blushing, remembering the total

breakdown of her inhibitions. How could making love with one man be a disaster, and with another a triumph? He had hurt her a little, yes. But long before that he had given her exquisite pleasure. In the end she had welcomed the moment of pain in order to be completely his, as close as two people could be.

She sat up and reached for her dress. 'Supposing someone had seen us?—trespassers, boys from the village.'

Reid pulled her into his arms, smoothing her hair, kissing her forehead and temples.

'I had a look round beforehand. There was no one lurking in the woods.'

'You planned it? You meant it to happen before you went for a walk?'

'We've been married almost a week. It couldn't be put off much longer. Sleeping alone in the dressing-room has been turning me into an insomniac, which I don't wish to be,' he said dryly.

'But last night I invited you to sleep with me, and you refused,' she reminded him.

'The circumstances weren't propitious. I preferred to take you by surprise, having first taken certain measures to undermine your defences.'

'Giving me lashings of champagne, do you mean?'

'No, champagne may lower a woman's resistance, but it doesn't heighten her responsiveness. The champagne was to make you sleepy. Sleeping in the sun is an aphrodisiac.'

'Is it?' she asked, in surprise. 'I didn't know that. How did you?'

Reid didn't answer her immediately. She was lying on her back again now. He was leaning over her, stroking her face with his fingertips.

'Probably I read it somewhere.'

But his hesitation made her guess that he hadn't read it. He must have been told it by a woman, one of the many who had preceded her, and with whom he was bound to compare her.

She wound her arms round his neck. 'You've been incredibly patient. I was so afraid ...' She paused, searching for the right words. '... I thought I must be frigid or something, but you made it wonderful for me. Thank you, Reid.' She reached up to kiss him.

'My pleasure, ma'am,' he said politely, his eyes laughing at her. Then his eyebrows contracted and he added, 'He must have been a fool or a brute to make you as scared as you were. Or was he also a novice?'

'No, I think he'd had scores of girls, but ... oh, I want to forget him. I can now. This was really the first time for me. The other was ... just a bad dream. Oh, Reid, I'm so happy ... so happy!'

She was. For some hours after that, she was happier than ever before. He had introduced her to a pleasure she had thought she would never experience. She was cured of an emotional disablement which, for two years, had blighted her life and scotched all her youthful dreams. Between gratitude and post-coital euphoria, she was floating on a cloud on which she was to remain for several days.

When Diana visited her mother for the first time since her wedding day, Lady Marriott said approvingly, 'How well you look ... quite transformed. All those weeks of worrying about me had taken it out of you, darling. I was getting quite worried about *you*. But now you look positively glowing.'

Diana knew that she did. Three days of Reid's wonderful lovemaking had made her bloom like a rose. She awoke in his arms and went to sleep in them, and in between he had taught her things about her body which were a revelation to her.

The patience he had shown at the outset of their honeymoon had changed to a seemingly insatiable desire. They made love at all hours of the day and night and, far from feeling exhausted, she felt more vitally alive than she could ever remember.

When she looked in the mirror she saw glossy hair and sparkling eyes. It was as if she had drunk a magic elixir which had changed her from a passably pretty girl into a beauty.

She had been with her mother an hour when Reid joined them. After he had kissed her and enquired how she was, Lady Marriott said, 'Diana has been telling me some of your exciting plans for the house.'

'Depending on your approval, Patience.'

She had asked him to use her first name in preference to any of the titles given to mothers-in-law, none of which she liked.

'Well, actually something has happened which makes my opinion rather irrelevant, my dears. I'm not coming back to the Abbey.'

'Not coming back!' Diana instantly assumed that her mother had taken it into her head that she would be an unwanted third in what should be a *ménage à deux*. 'That's perfectly ridiculous, Mummy. Of course you must live at the Abbey. It's your home . . . your place in the world. Why, for heaven's sake, that's the——' She stopped short.

Fortunately the silence which followed her bitten-off gaffe did not last more than two seconds.

Her mother said, 'No, dearest, not any more. It used to be my place in the world, but now there is somewhere else, or rather some*one* else who matters more to me.'

'You mean General Tarrant,' said Reid, in an unsurprised tone.

'Yes. Christopher has asked me to marry him. How clever of you to guess, Reid.'

'Not really. I noticed the way he looked at you at our wedding reception.'

Later, while they were having an early dinner at the flat before going to the theatre, Diana said, 'You never told me you suspected there might be another wedding in the offing.'

'No, I thought it best to say nothing. You were already in a panic about our sexual relationship. The idea that you might have agreed to our marriage unnecessarily could have been the last straw. As you almost said this afternoon, when your mother first broke her news to us, making it possible for her to live at the Abbey was the principal reason you married me.'

He was looking at his food as he spoke, and she couldn't tell what he was feeling. Perhaps he wasn't feeling anything, merely stating a fact—or what had been a fact at that time. But not any more.

I love him, she realised, aghast. It wasn't true on our wedding day. But it is now. I've fallen in love with him.

In the weeks which followed, Diana was constantly alert for the slightest sign that Reid might feel something more than he had at the time of his proposal. But although her devotion to him grew stronger the longer she lived with him, she watched in vain for any evidence that he cared for her more than he had before their honeymoon.

He was everything a husband should be—except that he never said he loved her. In a way, she minded that less than not being able to put her own love into words. She became more and more afraid of betraying herself, especially when she was in his arms. She felt that the moment he knew he had conquered her heart as well as her body, he would begin to be bored with her.

Throughout their first autumn at the Abbey, she was a fascinated witness to the extraordinary mental and physical energy which had enabled her husband to achieve his ambition of becoming a millionaire while still a young man.

She had expected it to take years to put the ancient fabric to rights, but it soon seemed that, under Reid's dynamic direction, the task would be accomplished quite quickly. As with any historic house, there would never be a time when some part of the Abbey was not under repair. But that, to a lesser extent, was true even of a recent building.

Together they ransacked the store-room filled with

relics of earlier generations which had subsequently
been discarded by their ancestors. Their search brought
to light many things of far finer quality than those in
use in the house.

While all this activity was going on, they were also
being invited to dine with the owners of other large
houses in the locality, and laying the foundations of
their social life. However, in spite of making new
friends, Diana continued to see a good deal of her first
friends in England, Val and Barney Lawrence.

As soon as she was discharged from the hospital,
Patience and Christopher were married. Like Reid and
Diana, they spent their honeymoon at home because,
for some time to come, it would be necessary for Lady
Marriott—as she still was technically, although she
wished in future to be known by her husband's name—
to have frequent checks at the hospital.

Although she talked to her mother two or three times
a week on the telephone, their relationship had been so
much closer than that of many mothers and daughters
that Diana could not help feeling a little bereft now
they saw so much less of each other.

She had lost Bertie too, in a way. No longer a frisky
puppy but a more sedate young dog, he had become
Reid's shadow now. He was still fond of her, but it was
Reid he followed everywhere unless told to stay. She
could understand his devotion. She felt the same way
herself.

One evening, after dinner, Reid astonished her by
saying, 'I think you should discourage young Lawrence
from spending so much of his time here.'

'Why?' Diana asked blankly. She had thought Reid
liked Barney Lawrence.

Having completed the work on his book about the
grounds of the Abbey, he had decided to try his hand at
some paintings of the interior. In this he had been
inspired by Turner, one of the greatest of all English
artists, who had painted several of the rooms as they
were in the early nineteenth century.

'Because I suspect he's in danger of falling in love

with you,' was her husband's answer to her question.

For some moments Diana was too startled to speak. She couldn't believe there was any foundation in the suggestion. Barney was entranced by the house, not by her.

'Am I so irresistible?' she asked, with a touch of coquetry.

Reid didn't respond to it. 'He's at a susceptible age,' was his damping reply.

Disappointed, she said, 'I don't see how I'm to stop him working here without offending him.'

'You needn't go as far as that. Just don't have your coffee breaks with him, or let him hang about after he's finished working. The other day he spent more time chatting to you than painting the cloister.'

It was true, but how did he know it? she wondered. Was it possible . . .?

'Are you jealous of him, Reid?' she asked lightly, putting her thought into words.

Reid gave her a glance which she couldn't interpret, then returned his attention to the *Financial Times* which he had been reading before raising the subject.

But Diana was not going to let it drop. 'To be jealous of Barney would be as absurd as my being jealous of Clementina,' she remarked. 'At least I *hope* it would be silly for me to be jealous of her.'

The pink pages of the newspaper rustled as he lowered it. 'Clementina?' he repeated, raising an eyebrow.

'I don't know her other name. I heard Sandro Oneto mention her as one of your many ex-lady-loves.'

Reid tossed the paper aside. Rising to his feet, he crossed the room to where she was sitting and, taking her hands, pulled her out of her chair.

'Where are we going?' she said, as he strode out of the library.

'When children are fractious, there's only one thing to be done with them. The same applies to women. Except that in their case——' throwing a quizzical glance over his shoulder '—one goes to bed with them.'

Which in its way, was a very satisfactory reaction to her attempt to needle him. But how long would his desire for her last? And how could she bear it when it waned?

CHAPTER SEVEN

DIANA enrolled for a course of pottery-making classes being held in the nearest small town because it was something she had always wanted to have a go at, and because she had read an article about the pottery at Holkham Hall in Norfolk.

This, started on a small scale by the Countess of Leicester in 1957, had grown into a business with over two thousand outlets in Britain and in many countries overseas.

It seemed to Diana that a pottery workshop ought have a place at the Abbey, but first she would try her own hand at it. She went every Thursday afternoon, using the east gate which, after being closed for years, now had its hinges oiled and its lock put in order to save her going and returning by way of the main gates. Using the east gate cut several miles off her journey.

On the afternoon of her fifth class, she drove home under a lowering sky which promised rain before nightfall. Outside the gate, she stopped the car and got out to open it. She was thinking about tea by the library fire when someone came up behind her and hooked their arms over hers, forcing her elbows together in the small of her back.

She gave a gasp of surprise and pain, but before she could cry out for help—not that anyone would have heard her for the lane was almost always deserted—a hideous, misshapen face appeared in front of her and slapped something sticky over her mouth, pressing it against her cheeks and chin. Then a cloth bag was pulled over her head and her wrists were lashed tightly together. She felt herself lifted and found herself hanging, head down, over someone's shoulder.

It all happened so fast that she didn't have a chance to struggle, and the gag of sticking plaster prevented her from uttering any sounds other than muffled moans.

She was still in a state of shock when she heard a vehicle draw up and she was bundled into it and thrown down on what felt like a pile of sacks. In less than a couple of minutes since leaving her own car, she was being driven away. But where, and by whom, she knew not. It was a few moments more before she understood fully what was happening.

She was being kidnapped.

There followed a period of time—how long she had no means of telling, but it seemed an eternity—in which she was more terrified than she had ever been in her life. Half-suffocated by the large piece of plaster effectively sealing her mouth, she knew that if she were sick—and, as she was discovering, the expression 'sick with fright' was based on physical fact—she would die of asphyxia.

As far as she could tell, she was in the back of an ancient rattletrap van. If there was anybody with her, they would not know she was choking to death. They would think her last sounds were merely incoherent protests.

Summoning all her will-power to combat the terror-stricken nausea which welled up inside her, she strove to inhale through her nose the deep breaths she needed to calm her—if anyone could be calm in such a horrific situation.

She knew that it could be some time before anyone at the Abbey began to worry about her. Reid was out for the afternoon, and might not return until six or later.

If she was not back for tea, the staff would conclude she was chatting to her fellow potters, perhaps had gone home with one of them. It was only when she failed to turn up in time to have her bath and change her clothes for the evening that Gwynneth, her maid, would become alarmed. Then either Reid would send someone out to look for her, thinking her car had broken down; or he would go out himself and find it abandoned.

But by then, even at the speed the van was travelling which did not seem to be very fast, she could be a hundred miles away.

Lying on her side with her arms pinioned behind her soon became acutely uncomfortable. All her weight seemed to be on her aching shoulder. Presently she rolled on to her front and lay with her head turned to one side, not in comfort but in less discomfort.

As the jolting journey continued, inevitably her thoughts turned to the fate of other people who had been kidnapped.

It was not a common crime in England, as it seemed to be in Italy and some other countries. In recent years, as far as she could remember, there had been only two cases. In one, a man who had murdered a judge had forced a passing motorist to drive him away from the scene of the crime, and had later tied him up in a wood and stolen the car. The motorist had survived unharmed, and the killer had been jailed for twenty-five years.

Similarly, in Ireland, a wealthy man held for ransom by terrorists hoping for funds with which to buy arms had eventually been released uninjured.

But a girl who had been kidnapped by a maniac had died in horrible circumstances, and it was of her wretched captivity and cruel death that Diana tried not to think as she lay on the foul-smelling sacks, every lurch and bump taking her further from everything she held dear and might never see again.

One grain of hope was that she was not in the hands of an unbalanced individual but of a gang whose motive for taking her was obviously money. She realised now that the horribly deformed features of the one who had gagged her had been caused by a nylon stocking pulled over his head to disguise him. On top of the stocking he had been wearing a Balaclava helmet. In the unlikely event of her being able to escape, she would not be able to give any description of him other than his height, which was about the same as her own in the flat-heeled shoes she was wearing.

Several times she thought they had reached their destination, only to find the stop was a temporary one—perhaps at traffic lights or T-junctions. But at last the journey came to an end and she heard the rear doors being thrown open.

The rough hands of more than one person heaved and hauled her out of the van and on to her feet. Supported on either side by the painful grip on her upper arm of a male hand, she was hustled forward, dazed and stumbling. A few moments later she was pushed into a sitting position on what felt like the edge of a bed, because there was a soft surface beneath her but nothing behind her. Footsteps crossed a hard floor. A door banged. She was alone.

Longing to tear off the bag and the loathsome gag, she began to try to free her wrists. But they were too securely bound by a thick cord for her to have any success.

Some more time passed. Then she heard the door open and, although she could hear only one pair of feet, she felt sure that several people—the others wearing soft-soled shoes—had re-entered the room.

A man's voice, young-sounding, uneducated, but without any recognisable accent, said, 'We're going to take off the gag so you can record a message for your husband. It's no use screaming—no one'll hear you. If you keep quiet, we'll leave the gag off. It's up to you. D'you understand?'

She nodded.

She expected them to remove the bag which covered her head and shoulders before they took off the gag, but one of them lifted the front of the bag, keeping her eyes covered, and another ripped off the plaster. It hurt her, but she didn't think it was an act of deliberate brutality. It would have been equally painful to have had it pulled away slowly.

'This is what you've got to say,' the voice told her.

' "This is Diana speaking. Nothing bad will happen to me if you do what he says. Don't go to the police—they'll never find me. If you want me back, do what he says." I'll say that again and you repeat it after me. "This is Diana speaking . ."

She listened, trying to moisten her lips which felt dry and numb after so long held in an unnatural position by the plaster.

'May I have some water to drink, please?' she asked hoarsely.

'Okay.'

After a short interval, the front of the bag was raised again and a glass was put to her mouth. It smelt as if it had held beer recently, and had not been rinsed out before being filled with heavily chlorinated tap water. She gulped down two or three mouthfuls.

'Thank you.' The habit of courtesy was too deeply ingrained for her not to be polite to her captors.

'Now we'll record the message,' said the man. 'Start when I tap your leg.'

There was nothing to be gained by refusing to do as she was told, and perhaps some good might come of it. Presumably they intended to play back the message on the telephone, perhaps in an isolated country kiosk. If, by the time they did that, Reid had already realised what had happened to her, it might be possible for him to have the call traced.

Anyway, if she refused to utter the message, they could easily make her obey them. People who went in for kidnapping would not scruple to use force upon her.

A hand tapped her knee and she repeated the message, trying to sound calm but unable to prevent her voice breaking as she said, 'If you want me back . . .'

When they left her alone again, she thought about Reid wanting her back. She felt sure that he would, but would he submit to extortion? She didn't think so.

She remembered a recent dinner party at which the conversation had turned to international terrorism. Her husband had expressed the view that the only way to stamp it out was never to give way to terrorists' demands, and to deal with convicted terrorists in the same way as with rabid dogs.

To which another man had said, 'That's easy to say, my dear chap, but if your wife or your mother were a hostage in terrorist hands, you would want to do anything to save them.'

'Not anything, George,' Reid had answered. 'An attempt at rescue —yes, fine. But agree to their terms— in no circumstances! Anyone who accedes to terrorists' demands is paving the way for another gang of thugs to try the same thing again. Ruthless men must be dealt with ruthlessly. If innocent victims get hurt or killed in the process, the blame lies with whoever didn't stand firm the last time such a thing happened.'

His uncompromising views had sparked off a lively argument, for even on this subject not everyone had been in agreement.

Diana had heard the woman sitting opposite her say to her neighbour, 'I think a man who put his duty to other people before his feelings for his wife would be a very odd, cold-blooded sort of husband, don't you?'

Reid was anything but cold-blooded, but he *was* an odd sort of husband. He wouldn't wish her to be harmed. He would do everything possible to have her found and rescued. But he wouldn't be prepared to pay an enormous ransom, of that she felt certain. Perhaps, if he had been desperately in love with her, he might have been. But he wasn't. Liking and desire were his feelings for her. And although, in combination, they might constitute a strong affection, they didn't add up to a love which would make a future without her impossible to contemplate. If she didn't survive this ordeal, he would soon replace her with someone else, she thought miserably.

Presently she heard what sounded like the van driving away. Wondering if she had been left alone in the house while her captors went to telephone the Abbey, she called out, 'Is anyone there? Can I speak to you, please?'

She was beginning to think she was alone when the

door opened and someone came in.

'What do you want?'

The voice wasn't that of the man who had spoken to her before.

'I'd like to go to the lavatory, please.'

There was silence. Perhaps there was no inside lavatory, and whoever had been left in charge of her was doubtful about allowing her to go to the outside privy.

'Come on, then.' She was seized by the arm and jerked to her feet.

'May I have my hands undone for a few minutes?' she asked, as she was led from the room.

Again there was no response. But after a door had been opened and she had been pushed forward, and then halted, she felt hands fumbling with the cord and was thankful that she wasn't going to be put through the humiliation of relieving herself under the supervision of a stranger.

Before she realised her hands were free, the door was slammed behind her and locked from the outside.

'Get a move on,' she was ordered.

As fast as she could for her fingers were clumsy from having their circulation impaired by the tightly fastened cord, she dragged off the bag and blinked in the seemingly brilliant glare of an unshaded bulb hanging from the narrow ceiling.

High up in the wall behind the lavatory pan was a window, partially open. Stepping on to the rim of the pan, which had neither a lid nor a seat, she peered out. There was not very much to be seen because the top-hung little window was held in place by a stay which she dared not lift from the peg in case it gave a squeak which would be heard by her guard.

Not that she could try to get out through the window. It was far too small. But he might be annoyed with her for looking out, especially as something she could see was the back wheel of a powerful motorbike parked behind some sort of outhouse.

Mentally repeating the bike's registration number to

fix it firmly in her memory, she stepped down and used the lavatory.

There was a bang on the door which made her jump. 'Hurry up, can't you?'

When, soon afterwards, she called out, 'I'm ready,' he told her to replace the bag and stand with her back to the door and her hands behind her.

For a while afterwards she felt somewhat heartened by the fact that she now had a clue to the identity of her captors. But whether she would ever be able to make use of it seemed doubtful.

She wondered how soon Reid would break the news to her mother, and what effect it would have on her. Even though Patience now had a perfectly sound heart, the shock and distress of having her daughter kidnapped must be bad for her so soon after a major operation.

Time seemed to pass very slowly with nothing to do but sit in the darkness and wonder what was happening at the Abbey, what Reid had been told to do, and whether he would obey the instruction not to contact the police.

At last she heard the van returning, and a few minutes later the door opened and she heard the light being switched on.

'I've brought you something to eat,' said the voice of the man who had dictated the message to her. 'Stand up. I'll undo your hands.'

He did not tell her to wait, but she didn't attempt to remove the bag until she had heard him go out and lock the door behind him. A parcel wrapped in newspaper was on the table in the centre of the room. It proved to contain fish and chips in a polystyrene dish. They had been liberally sprinkled with malt vinegar and salt, which Diana didn't take. But as her watch showed eight-fifteen, and she had had nothing to eat since a light salad lunch, she was grateful for any kind of food, even fish coated in a rather nasty yellow batter.

Before she had finished eating, he came back with a mug of something. His features were distorted by the stocking pulled over them, and his clothes were those of a million young men—patched jeans in need of being laundered and a black leather jacket ornamented with fringes and studs, worn over a denim jacket and a tee-shirt.

As he put the mug on the table, with a chocolate bar beside it, she noticed that his hands would have been attractive had the nails not been rimmed with machine oil and the two first fingers heavily stained with nicotine. On the middle finger was a silver ring in the form of a skull.

'Did you get through to my husband?' she asked him.

He ignored the question, and said, 'You're not used to eating with your fingers, are you?'

He spoke with contemptuous derision, and perhaps a hint of resentment. She thought she heard in his tone the grudge of a man who feels animosity towards anyone more fortunate than himself.

'You're not making much fuss, I'll say that for you.'

'It wouldn't do any good, would it? Why don't you let me go? You don't know my husband. I do. He won't pay whatever you're asking; he'll make it the reward for catching you. If you let me go now—dump me somewhere where I'll have a long walk to get help—you can get away scot free.'

'We'll do that anyway,' he answered. 'And your old man'll pay the money. If not we'll have to send him some presents. For a start, we'll send him your hair, and then we'll move on to your teeth. He'll come round to our way of thinking. Don't worry, darlin'. There's some very good wigs about, if you've got the money, and you'll look just as pretty with dentures.'

With a laugh he went out of the room, leaving Diana to wonder if he meant his threats, or was just trying to frighten her. The thought of losing her teeth was as horrifying to her as the loss of a finger or toe. Her courage wilted. She grasped the mug of hot tea with hands that shook.

It was strong and unpalatably sweet to someone who didn't take sugar. But she forced herself to drink it in the hope that it would steady her nerves.

The chocolate bar she left untouched. She already felt slightly queasy from the unaccustomed greasiness of the chips. Earlier, while she was eating them, she had looked round the sparsely furnished room and noticed the boarded-up windows which suggested the house had been empty for a long time.

When she heard the key in the lock, she was sitting with her head in her hands, filled with bitter regret that she had never told Reid how much she loved him.

Before the door opened, she straightened, squaring her shoulders and trying to look calm and composed.

This time he had brought her some pills.

'What are they?' she asked.

'Stuff to make you sleep. They won't hurt you.'

Reluctantly she picked up the three coloured capsules he had put on the table. She thought they were probably barbiturates, and she didn't want to take them. On the other hand, it wouldn't help her to spend all night awake, tossing and turning.

'If I take these, can I keep my hands free?'

'That's the idea. You take them and we know you're out cold and won't give no trouble.'

When she had swallowed the capsules, he told her to lie on the bed, which consisted of an old and stained mattress with an equally ancient pillow and a folded khaki blanket.

She was shaking out the blanket when he switched off the light and closed the door.

Being in the dark again made her realise that, if the house was empty and derelict, the power would have been cut off. Unless, being particularly isolated, it had its own generator which the gang had managed to put to use.

As she lay down and covered herself, she thought of her own comfortable bed where tonight Reid would sleep on his own—if he went to bed at all. Again, she wished with all her heart that she had admitted her love for him.

She saw now it had been pride which had kept her

silent. She had not been ready to admit her total
dependence on him when he didn't feel the same way.
But now that she was in danger—for who knew what
these people were capable of if things didn't go as they
planned—pride seemed a trivial consideration. If she
came through this dreadful experience, the first thing
she would tell him was how much he meant to her.

Afterwards, she could never remember very clearly
the events of that night. They were as confused as a bad
dream. She remembered being brought to the surface of
an unnaturally deep sleep and, only half awake, hustled
outside to the van where she lay on the sacks, not
caring where they were taking her because her mind was
so fuddled by the heavy dose of sleeping pills.

Some time later she was roused again and made to
get out, shivering in the sharp night air against which
her jersey and trousers—she had left her mac in the
car—offered little protection.

The next thing she knew was that she was standing in
a country lane and the van was driving away from her,
its headlamps illuminating the hedgerows until it turned
a corner and left her in darkness, listening to the sound
of its engine fading away in the distance.

There was no moon that night, or stars. She was as
blind as if she still had the bag over her head. But
apparently she was free again. They seemed to have
done what she had suggested—dumped her in the
middle of nowhere and got to hell out of it.

In the ordinary way she might have been frightened
at being out on her own, in the middle of the night, in
countryside she didn't know. But in present circumstances her only fear was that the men might change
their minds and come back for her.

She wanted to put as much distance between herself
and the place where they had dropped her as she could.
But without a torch she couldn't walk away, let alone
run. For all she knew, the lane might lead to a quarry
or a gravel pit now filled with water, or to some other
hazard.

The best thing she could do was to edge her way

carefully forward till she reached the field gate she had seen fifty yards further on. If she could find it in the dark, she could climb it and hide in the field until either the night sky cleared and there was enough starlight to see by, or until the first grey light of day crept over the landscape.

It took her a long time, but by sliding one foot in front of the other on the hard surface of the lane—and thanking heaven for England's incomparable network of tarred byroads—she found her way to the gate. It was easy enough to climb it, not so easy to make her way along the inner side of the hedge.

When she thought she must be out of sight of the van if it drove back that way, she sank down upon the damp earth and prepared for a long, cold vigil. Although she felt perished at first, after a while the powerful sedatives they had given her began to make her sleepy again.

She woke up to find herself lying on the ground, in daylight, with a worried-looking man staring down at her.

As she sat up, groaning a little at the stiffness of her neck and back, he said, 'You gave me a proper scare, missy—lying there as if you were dead. You will be dead before long sleeping in the open without even a coat on. Asking for trouble, that is.'

'I don't make a habit of it.' Diana got to her feet. 'I'm sorry I gave you a fright, but it's nothing to the one I've had. Where's the nearest telephone, please? I must make an urgent call as quickly as possible.'

'Mr and Mrs Bailey have a telephone. I daresay they'd let you use it for something important. Lea Cottage . . . a mile down the lane.'

'Thank you.' She made for the gate.

Her head ached. Her whole body ached. But she felt on top of the world, and she couldn't wait to speak to Reid.

It seemed a very long mile. She ran some of the way, walked the rest.

The elderly man who answered her rap on the doorknocker was still in his dressing gown and pyjamas.

'Yes?' he said, not looking too pleased at the sight of a strange girl on his doorstep before nine o'clock.

'I'm sorry to disturb you, Mr Bailey, but I need to make a call to the police, and a farm-worker told me to come here.'

'By all means. Come in. The telephone is in the sitting-room.' Without waiting to close the door after her, he led her to it.

By the time she had been connected to the nearest police station and explained who she was, and where she was ringing from, Mr Bailey's wife had appeared to stand beside him and listen with a horrified face to what Diana told the police.

'Now may I please ring my husband and tell him I'm safe?' she asked them, when the first call was finished.

'Certainly ... yes, do, by all means,' said Mr Bailey.

'The poor man ... he must be frantic!' was his wife's sympathetic comment, as she watched Diana dial the operator and then ask her to put through a reverse charge call to the Abbey.

It was Reid's valet who answered the telephone.

'Anderson, this is Mrs Lockwood. I'm free—they've let me go. Is my husband there?'

'Oh, that's wonderful news, Mrs Lockwood! Mr Lockwood's just taking a shower, but I'll fetch him at once.'

However, Reid must have heard the telephone ringing. She heard Anderson say, 'It's your wife. She's safe, sir,' and then a deeper voice rasped, 'Diana? Where are you?'

'I'm with a Mr and Mrs Bailey who are letting me use their telephone. I'm safe and I'm well, and if you'll hold on a minute, I'll ask them where I am.' She was half laughing, half in tears.

Mr Bailey took the receiver from her. 'This is John Bailey speaking, Mr Lockwood.' He gave Reid his address and telephone number, adding, 'Your wife has already been in touch with the local police who, I gather, are sending a car round. In the meantime my wife and I will take every care of her. Considering what she's been through, she's looking amazingly perky. Now I'll hand you back to her.'

'Reid, does Mummy know?' she asked anxiously. 'If so, I must ring her at once.'

'No, she doesn't know yet. I was going to have to tell her eventually, but I was putting it off as long as possible.'

'Thank heavens you did! She would have been out of her mind with worry.'

'As we all were. Are you really all right? That brute hasn't hurt you?'

'No, no—I'm fine. A bit fuddled from being doped with sleeping pills and spending part of the night in a field, but otherwise I'm in great shape. I don't suppose you had much sleep last night.'

'None,' was his succinct reply. 'Why did they let you go?'

'I don't know. I can't understand it. But although where I am now may be a long way from where they were holding me, I do have one clue which may help the police to track them down. They'll want to ask me a lot of questions, I expect. I don't know what time it may be before I get home.'

'I'll come to you. I'll be there—at the police station— as soon as I can. I can't wait to see for myself that you really are safe,' said Reid, his voice rather ragged.

The Baileys had discreetly withdrawn. There was no one but her husband to hear her say softly, 'I can't wait to see you either. I love you very much, Reid. I don't think I realised how much till last night when I thought I might never see you again. Goodbye. Drive carefully, darling.'

Quickly she replaced the receiver, so that he shouldn't be embarrassed by being unable to respond to her declaration.

She was glad she had told him how she felt. It was like a great weight off her shoulders. From now on there would be no more pretending. All her responses would be honest ones.

*To thine own self be true ... thou canst not then be
false to any man*—Shakespeare had written in *Hamlet*.

By hiding her love for him from Reid, she had been
false to herself, with all the mental unease attendant on
living a lie, or even a half-truth.

When she went into the hall, Mrs Bailey was coming
down the stairs. Like her husband, she was still in her
nightclothes under a cosy quilted dressing gown.

'My dear, I've run a hot bath. I think you should
have one at once. Then I'll lend you some clothes
belonging to my younger daughter who still lives at
home when she's not away at university.'

'It's terribly kind of you. A bath would be heaven. I
feel such a mess,' said Diana.

'I should think so too, you poor thing! The
bathroom's the first on the left at the top of the stairs.
You'll see I've put out a new toothbrush and a tube of
paste, and also a new comb. I always have one in
reserve.'

Much as she would have liked to lie soaking in the
Baileys' bath until the water began to cool, Diana did
not linger in it. She guessed it would not be long before
the police arrived.

She was drying herself on a large towel warmed by a
hot rail when Mrs Bailey came up to tell her there was a
police car at the gate. Six or seven minutes later,
wearing a skirt and jersey belonging to Miss Bailey, she
went downstairs to find two plain clothes police officers
in the sitting-room.

'Mrs Lockwood must have a cup of tea and
something to eat before she leaves here,' Mrs Bailey
said firmly, when they had introduced themselves.

To Diana's astonishment, one was the Chief
Constable of the police force of the area, and the other
was a Chief Inspector.

'By all means,' agreed the Chief Constable. 'But
perhaps you wouldn't mind answering some questions
while you have breakfast, Mrs Lockwood. Time is of
the essence in a case of this nature, you understand.'

Diana nodded. 'I think the most important thing I

can tell you is the number of the motorbike which was outside the house where they took me.'

He and the Inspector exchanged a swift glance.

'That's a piece of luck we didn't expect,' said the Inspector. 'What was the number, Mrs Lockwood?'

Having jotted it down, he went out to the waiting police car.

Thus it was that, within an hour, by which time Diana had said goodbye to the Baileys and thanked them for their kind hospitality, and had been driven to the local police headquarters, some light was already being thrown on the mystery of her sudden release from captivity. 'It appears that one of your captors has already had his come-uppance,' the Chief Constable told her, when he joined her in his comfortable office, to which she had been taken by a policewoman. 'Shortly before midnight, he was in collision with a car, not far from a lorry-drivers' pull-in which is a meeting place for several gangs of the Hell's Angels type. He's now in a critical condition in hospital.'

The Inspector, who had followed his superior into the room, said, 'It seems probable that he went to the café to establish an alibi. It may be that there were other motorbikes at the house which you didn't see; and that the reason you were heavily sedated was so that all those involved in the kidnapping could spend some time at the café last night.'

'Our theory, for the time being,' continued the Chief Constable, 'is that when the other members of the gang witnessed the accident in which their leader was seriously injured, they panicked. Perhaps he had reported to them your suggestion about letting you go, and, in the circumstances, they saw it as their best course of action.'

Presently Diana demurred to their suggestion that it might be advisable for her to have a medical check. Now, feeling completely herself again, except for being tired, she thought it unnecessary.

'Are there any more formalities, Chief Constable? When my husband arrives, I should like to be free to leave with him as soon as possible.'

'Naturally. No, apart from asking you to sign the statement we took from you earlier, we needn't detain you,' he answered. 'May I say how much I admire your remarkably cool, calm behaviour, Mrs Lockwood. I'm quite sure that none of our women officers, who are trained to handle unpleasant situations, could have behaved with greater good sense and fortitude than you've shown in the last eighteen hours.'

'Thank you, but I was very scared under the surface,' Diana confessed.

There was a tap at the door, and a young police constable opened it.

'Mr Lockwood, sir,' he announced.

Reid strode rapidly over the threshold, stopping short at the sight of his wife rising from the chair by the desk. She had never seen him look so tired. His lean face was haggard with strain.

'Oh, Reid . .'

As she moved towards him, he strode forward again to grasp her outstretched hands in his.

'My darling girl . . . my dear love . . .' he said, in a rough, husky voice.

As her lips trembled, and she strove not to burst into tears of joy at the sight of him, she was astonished to see a sudden bright glaze in his eyes, and the violent clenching of his jaw as he fought for control of his feelings.

Then, ignoring the two men with her, he crushed her in a fierce bear-hug, his face buried in her soft hair, his body trembling with emotion.

By the time they emerged from that first convulsive embrace, they had the room to themselves. As their lips met, she felt as if they were kissing each other for the first time, not with passion but with infinite tenderness.

When Reid lifted his head and produced a handkerchief with which to dry her wet cheeks she knew that the moisture glistening on his was not all from her eyes.

Reid, the hard, tough, self-possessed man she had thought a stranger to love, had been moved to tears by having her safely restored to him.

'I love you,' he murmured. 'Oh, how I love you, Diana! You are all the loves of my life, the first love I never experienced—the last and best love, my darling. Can you forgive my stupidity in not telling you before?'

'I could forgive you anything,' she answered softly. 'I can even forgive those men now, because if this hadn't happened I might have gone on being afraid to tell you how happy you've made me ... what a wonderful lover you are ... how I longed and longed for you to love me.'

'As I do, and have for some time ... since before we were married,' he told her. 'But I thought you were still in love with the man you once told me about.'

'No! Why did you think that?'

'A girl like you doesn't give herself lightly. And they say a woman never forgets her first lover.'

She slid her arms round his neck. 'She never forgets the first man who ... flies her to the stars. For me that was you, Reid. I was never truly a woman until our picnic in the park. And even that, lovely as it is, is only a little part of what a woman wants from a man. You've given me all the other things. Your care and protection when my mother was in hospital. Your help in keeping the Abbey going. And ... oh, a score of little things. A smile across the room at a party ... rescue when I'm stuck with a bore ... I could go on forever.'

There was a tap at the door and, after a tactful interval to allow them to draw apart, the Chief Constable came in.

After making himself known to Reid, he said, 'The statement is ready for your signature now, Mrs Lockwood. You have only to read it through to check that it's correct, and then your husband can take you home. I expect you'd like to read a copy of your wife's account of her experience, Mr Lockwood.'

'I certainly should. Is there any hope of catching those swine?'

'A very good chance we shall arrest the whole lot of them.'

As it wasn't far out of their way, Diana prevailed on Reid to stop at a florist's shop to buy a bouquet of red roses for Mrs Bailey which she would deliver in person. He was not averse to calling to thank the little woman for her part in his wife's misadventure; but at the same time he wanted to get Diana home as soon as possible, to put her to bed to rest and recover from her experience.

'I don't mind being put to bed ... if you come with me,' she said.

For the first time that day, he grinned. 'We'll have to see about that!'

During most of the journey back, after calling briefly on the Baileys to whom she would post the clothes she had borrowed, they discussed the kidnapping. Diana suspected that from now on he would either insist on driving her everywhere himself, or depute someone else to chauffeur her.

'I wonder why they picked me out?' she said.

'Probably as a result of a paragraph about us in one of the tabloids. Who knows what inspires thugs and maniacs to act as they do? Last night I was going crazy, thinking of you shut up with some vicious hooligan who might take it into his head to rape you.' He took his eyes off the road for an instant to look at her. 'Bacon never wrote anything more true than *He that hath wife and children hath given hostages to fortune*.'

When they arrived at the Abbey, Diana was surprised and moved by the warmth of feeling expressed by everyone she encountered. In a household formed only recently, she had not expected the staff to be more than ordinarily concerned about her. But it seemed they had all shared in Reid's night of frantic anxiety.

When she expressed her surprise, he said, 'You're a very lovable person, Diana. There's something about you that touches people's hearts.'

They were upstairs in her sitting-room, and Watson, Ratty's successor, had just left the room after bringing a bottle of Pol Roger 1973. On the way home, Reid had used the telephone in his car to ask the butler to put some champagne on ice as a pick-me-up for Diana, and for everyone else at the Abbey to drink to her safe return.

'I knew I had a corner of Bertie's heart,' she said, fondling her dog's silky ears as he rested his muzzle on her lap, his black tail lashing back and forth, 'but I wasn't sure you possesed one.

'It wasn't that you weren't kind to me,' she went on. 'In most ways you were the perfect husband. But I wanted words as well as deeds. Perhaps men don't need to be told they're loved, but women do. The act of love, however wonderful, isn't enough. We need to hear the words "I love you"—and to be able to say them, which I never felt I could. I thought you might find me a bore if I let on how much I loved you. Although I should have thought you would have guessed it from the way I melted whenever you touched me.'

'On the contrary, there were times when I thought I was making things worse for myself by being able to draw a response from you,' said Reid, looking down at her from a standing position while she sat on the chaise-longue with her feet up. 'Sometimes, after we'd spent half the night making love, I felt you actually disliked me for teaching you things which you didn't want to learn—or not from me,' he added, with a rueful half smile.

'Oh, no,' she protested. 'I was only embarrassed at having been so ... abandoned. Sometimes you would look at me across the breakfast table, and your eyes would be amused, and I would feel horribly shy. It was never *dislike*. I—I like the things you've taught me. Who wouldn't?'—blushing and smiling at the same time.

Reid laughed. The chaise-longue was a wide one and there was plenty of room for him to sit beside her, facing her.

'You've taught me things, too, my sweet one. I realise now that in love, as in other arts, it's not enough to have knowledge and technique. There has to be feeling as well. Before he settles down, a man may often want to go to bed with a woman. But to want to sleep with her in the literal sense, and to wake up with her—that's something else.'

He put his glass on the table near the chaise and then he placed her glass beside it. Finally he put his arms round her and began very gently, to kiss her. She snuggled against him with a wordless murmur of delight at being safely back in his arms, with all her doubts about their future resolved.

Presently, when he continued to hold her as if she were made of eggshell porcelain, she drew back a little, saying, 'I'm not an invalid, darling. You're holding me as if I might break!'

Then she took his face between her hands and gave him a slow, sensuous kiss until his arm crushed her close, and his mouth took command of hers, making her tremble with pleasure.

Soon he picked her up and carried her through the connecting door to the bedroom where he put her on the bed. When he had shut Bertie out, and locked all the doors, he came back to the bed and undressed, the sight of his long muscular back making her reach out her hand to stroke the smooth warmth of his skin. It felt like an expensive kid glove.

At her touch, half-undressed, he turned, his grey eyes dark with desire. It was as if they had been separated for much longer than a night and part of a day; as if they had been apart for weeks. Which, in a way, they had.

Diana sat up and pulled off her jersey. As she tugged it over her head, she felt his hands unclip her bra. A few seconds later she was bare to the waist, her soft torso pressed to his hard one, her slender arms locked round his neck.

'I love you, Diana,' he told her huskily.

'I love you,' she echoed.

When, much later, she lay, exhausted and drowsy, her body relaxed beneath his, and her mind at peace, she had an intuitive conviction that, not too long after the end of their first year together, she would have the first of his children.

Harlequin® Plus

A WORD ABOUT THE AUTHOR

Although Anne Weale and her husband are British, they have lived for the past five years in a Spanish villa perched on a clifftop above the Costa Blanca—Spain's beautiful "white coast." From her desk in a corner of the drawing room she enjoys a wide view of miles of Mediterranean coastline.

Anne and her husband are world travelers, and recent destinations have included Florida, New England, Italy and the Caribbean. A constant companion is Anne's portable typewriter. More than once she has been tempted to start tapping the keys in the middle of the night!

Actually, Anne feels a book is improved if there is time to mull over the first flash of inspiration for a few weeks before putting it to paper. Also, there is usually a great deal of background reading to be done, as well as on-the-spot research. This involves talking to as many of the local inhabitants as possible, spending hours in the local-history section of the library and generally seeing everything there is to be seen.

Anne's husband is an invaluable help to her with her writing. She explains that his viewpoint coincides with the hero's. While she disappears downtown to explore the shops, he may head for some historic fortification. His impressions and observations of his excursions have found their place in many of her novels.

Anne Weale began her writing career as a journalist but gave up journalism to follow her husband to the Far East. Out of her first two years of living in an exotic land came *Winter Is Past* (Romance #582), set in Malaysia—the first of more than fifty books by this favorite Harlequin author.

HARLEQUIN
PREMIERE AUTHOR EDITIONS

6 top Harlequin authors—6 of their best books!

1. JANET DAILEY Giant of Mesabi
2. CHARLOTTE LAMB Dark Master
3. ROBERTA LEIGH Heart of the Lion
4. ANNE MATHER Legacy of the Past
5. ANNE WEALE Stowaway
6. VIOLET WINSPEAR The Burning Sands

Harlequin is proud to offer these 6 exciting romance novels by 6 of our most popular authors. In brand-new beautifully designed covers, each Harlequin Premiere Author Edition is a bestselling love story—a contemporary, compelling and passionate read to remember!

Available in September wherever paperback books are sold, *or* through Harlequin Reader Service. Simply complete and mail the coupon below.

- -

Take these 4 best-selling novels FREE

as advertised on TV

Yes! Four sophisticated, contemporary love stories by four world-famous authors of romance FREE, as your introduction to the Harlequin Presents subscription plan. Thrill to **Anne Mather**'s passionate story BORN OUT OF LOVE, set in the Caribbean.... Travel to darkest Africa in **Violet Winspear**'s TIME OF THE TEMPTRESS....Let **Charlotte Lamb** take you to the fascinating world of London's Fleet Street in MAN'S WORLD....Discover beautiful Greece in **Sally Wentworth**'s moving romance SAY HELLO TO YESTERDAY.

Harlequin Presents...

The very finest in romance fiction

Join the millions of avid Harlequin readers all over the world who delight in the magic of a really exciting novel. EIGHT great NEW titles published EACH MONTH! Each month you will get to know exciting, interesting, true-to-life people .... You'll be swept to distant lands you've dreamed of visiting .... Intrigue, adventure, romance, and the destiny of many lives will thrill you through each Harlequin Presents novel.

Get all the latest books before they're sold out!

As a Harlequin subscriber you actually receive your personal copies of the latest Presents novels immediately after they come off the press, so you're sure of getting all 8 each month.

Cancel your subscription whenever you wish!

You don't have to buy any minimum number of books. Whenever you decide to stop your subscription just let us know and we'll cancel all further shipments.

Your FREE gift includes

Anne Mather—Born out of Love
Violet Winspear—Time of the Temptress
Charlotte Lamb—Man's World
Sally Wentworth—Say Hello to Yesterday

FREE Gift Certificate
and subscription reservation

Mail this coupon today!

Harlequin Reader Service

In the U.S.A.
1440 South Priest Drive
Tempe, AZ 85281

In Canada
649 Ontario Street
Stratford, Ontario N5A 6W2

Please send me my 4 Harlequin Presents books free. Also, reserve a subscription to the 8 new Harlequin Presents novels published each month. Each month I will receive 8 new Presents novels at the low price of $1.75 each [*Total—$14.00 a month*]. There are no shipping and handling or any other hidden charges. I am free to cancel at any time, but even if I do, these first 4 books are still mine to keep absolutely FREE without any obligation. SB613

Offer expires January 31, 1984

NAME	(PLEASE PRINT)
ADDRESS	APT. NO.
CITY	
STATE/PROV.	ZIP/POSTAL CODE

If price changes are necessary you will be notified.

Introducing...

Harlequin American Romance

An exciting new series of sensuous and emotional love stories—contemporary, engrossing and uniquely American. Long, satisfying novels of conflict and challenge, stories of modern men and women dealing with life and love in today's changing world.